STEPHANIE JANE O'NEIL

On The Market

Contents

Chapter One

February 21st

Being at the end of my twenties definitely has its pros and cons.

It's been one day, thirteen hours, and five minutes since I turned twenty-nine, and as I sit on my stupidly expensive, velvet sofa, feeling the effects of last night's party, I go through said pros and cons in my head.

Pro: I'm a successful marketing executive, doing very well for myself.

Con: I'm still single, wasting money on expensive bottles of wine, and sitting alone in my flat every Friday night.

Pro: No more pros.

Con: Still single.

Extra con: Madilyn is getting married in nine months, and if I don't bring a date to the wedding, I'll officially be the disappointment of the family.

As I stare at my list, the cons weighing heavily on my mind, I begin writing on the back of a takeaway menu everything that I *will* change by the time I turn The Big 3-0. Starting with:

1. *I will stop going to all weddings without a date.*

The truth is, I no longer have the energy to deal with the constant questions—at every wedding I attend—regarding my very dull, depressing, and to be honest, non-existent love life. Not to mention all the dating advice which is forced down my throat, along with the wedding cake and copious amounts of alcohol needed just to sit through one hour of that torture.

1. *I will read more books, especially the ones already on my shelf, covered in the dust of my roaring twenties.*
2. *I will not drink two bottles of wine on a Friday evening whilst endlessly—pointlessly—scrolling through shopping sites, wasting money on embarrassingly unneeded lingerie.*
3. *I will start donating to charity more often. And to start, I'm going to sort through the clothes I haven't worn in over five years.*
4. *I will not turn my nose up at disgusting food. Being thirty means I must like everything and be mature. Even if that means I eat mushrooms...*

I sigh, scribbling out the last sentence as the thought of the vegetable I equate with actual garbage enters my mind.

I don't *have* to eat mushrooms to be mature, right?

Finally, I force my hand to write out one final change. The most important, and the one I am most unnerved by.

1. *I will try more with my love life.*

I want something more than just a date for a wedding I don't really care about.

I'm not the kind of woman who needs a man. I've reached the ripe old age of twenty-nine as a single woman, and I've done just fine. I know I've done well without a man, despite the expectations of … well, everyone.

But even though I don't *need* a man, I've reached the age where I'm fulfilled in every aspect of my life, *except* when it comes to love. My love life is a bottomless pit of nothingness—showing no signs of revival—buried deep within the earth where no one can dig it up.

Until now.

Until I received the gold-tinted invitation to, yet another, wedding that I would inevitably go to—dateless. The thought of attending another wedding without a man on my arm and having to endure the judgments of my family is enough to warrant a change. My cousin Madilyn is getting married to the love of her life, Sophia. And as I sit, staring at the gold-tinted invitation that screams love, I know that it's now or never. I need to change my love life from "non-existent" to "very much alive" in less than ten months.

I don't want to blame my lack of a love life on the fact that there are practically zero eligible bachelors where I live—though that's a massive factor. When I walk out of my flat, I see men who have more muscle than brain cells, and guys who have tattooed "YOLO" on their neck.

No thanks.

I place the takeaway menu down, hearing a very annoying, high-pitched, whiny laugh, barrelling down the hall outside my flat. A sudden, clunking sound follows, so, rolling my eyes to the point of dizziness, I place my wine down on my

3

custom-made, "*I love wine*" coaster and force myself off of the sofa.

Before I reach the window, I know who it'll be. I don't need to check the time to see that it's nearing midnight. Instead, I peek from the safety of my curtains, and watch as Lucas and a woman stumble into his flat, right next door to mine—like clockwork. His door is semi-obstructed from view, but I can see enough.

I roll my eyes, again.

It's the same thing, every Friday night—without fail—for a year. I tried really hard to ignore him, but there's only so much one can do when you're doomed to listen to the soundtrack of his headboard on repeat. Sometimes, I find myself thinking about where he finds these women. Is there an exclusive dating club down town I'm unaware of? If so, how does one join? That would make this whole dating situation a lot easier.

My laptop pings, announcing an incoming Face Time, and I realise I've been staring at Lucas's closed flat door for far too long. Shaking my head at myself and wrapping the silk shawl tighter around my shoulders, I settle back onto the sofa and answer.

"Rosie, I need your expertise. I know it's super late, but this is an actual, real-life emergency," Madilyn blurts.

I frown, noticing her eyes are red and blotchy. Usually when she calls me I'm greeted with, "Hey, Bitch," before she dives into the latest drama. This though—this feels different—and I prepare myself for what I know is coming.

"Shoot," I say, my mind now focused on my friend. Maddy is biting her fingernails as she considers her wording for a moment. I lean back onto the sofa, picking up my wine, as I know I'm in for a long night of talking down and reassurance.

I don't mind, though. I'm her ears, and she's mine. "What happened?" I ask, hoping it's not over between them.

"Sophia and I had another fight after your party last night. It was so stupid, but I think it's over." Worry and a deep sadness replace her usual witty demeanour as her voice cracks.

"What was it about?" I ask, already knowing the answer to my question.

"The usual"—she pauses, rubbing her head and taking a deep breath—"the fact I can't trust and I'm constantly worried about being heartbroken again. I don't know why I'm like this. I want to marry her, but I think I'm too broken," she whispers, tears threatening to fall from her eyes.

"You know why you do it, and it's normal. It's not ideal, but it's normal. You've been hurt over and over, so your mind is wired for that precise pattern," I try to explain. "But you need to try to trust Sophia—especially now that you're engaged. It's about time you open up to someone. Focus on her and the wedding, and everything else should fall into place."

She sniffles and wipes her eyes. I give her the best, reassuring smile I can muster, knowing she's coming around. "I know it's hard, but I also know you're the strongest bitch I've ever met. Call her." I take a sip of my wine, knowing it's not over between them. Sophia is super understanding, and to be honest, one of the best women I've had the pleasure of knowing.

"You know, you've always been the best at relationship advice. Maybe you should take your own advice and let someone in," she insists, wiping her tears, the sadness already starting to evaporate from her face.

"Those that can't do, teach," I say, hoping she will drop the subject.

"Come on, Rosie. Let's set you up. You're almost thirty, so

5

now is the best time! You can have a date for the wedding!" she exclaims, her problems with Sophia gone, and replaced with the need to satisfy my love life.

"You know I've never been good at dating. It's just not in my genes." I sit forward on the sofa, placing the laptop on the coffee table. As I do, the takeaway menu falls to the floor.

I pick it up, my eyes instantly landing on my last resolution: *I will try more with my love life.* I also take a glance towards the wedding invitation shining like a beacon on my coffee table, reminding me of the impending wedding day: *August 1st.*

If I don't try now, I will inevitably be alone for the rest of my life. At that thought, I envision my life and I can practically smell the catnip and hear the hundreds of blankets being knitted by yours truly. Despite my nerves, I know I know I have to do it.

"Let's do it." As I hear myself utter those words, I chug the remainder of my wine. My stomach flips and my heart starts beating faster.

Madilyn squeals and vacates the screen before coming back with a notepad and a pen.

"I've been waiting for this moment," she says, scribbling something down. It's true. She's been asking and begging for me to put myself out there, but it's always been a firm no. I was too focused on my career and my goals, but I need to be ready now.

"What are you doing?" I ask.

"I'm making a list of all the dating sites we're going to set you up on. Trust me, that's where the fish are swimming."

"Okay, I guess we can give them a go." I'm reluctant, but I trust her.

"That's the spirit! Let's get you a profile set up. Pick a few sexy, delicious, and irresistible photos for your profile," she says, typing erratically. Pulling my phone out, I do as she says. This will be less painful if I just give in.

As I'm scrolling through my photos, I find a picture that I completely forgot about. I'm standing in my blue and red graduation gown, smiling in a way I haven't done or seen in years. My hair was long and blonde in this picture, but since then, I've dyed it red and adopted a chic, shorter length.

"What about these?" I ask, putting my phone in front of my laptop camera. I can see Madilyn making faces of disdain as I swipe through my chosen pictures.

"What?" I ask, pulling my phone away and looking at the photos to see what was so wrong with them. I honestly don't see anything wrong with them—they're respectable, smart, and, in my opinion, sexy photos. In one of the pictures, I'm wearing my best grey suit, preparing for an interview for the job I have now. It's safe to say that suit is the reason I got the job.

"They're just too…" She pauses, thinking of her next words. "Boring…" she mutters, looking down and still typing something so fast, I'm afraid she'll break the keyboard.

"What? They're some of my best photos!" I object, not about to just take this criticism. "Just because I'm not half naked and wearing a thong, doesn't mean these photos are any less sexy! I'm a businesswoman."

"Rosie, just trust me, okay?" she pleads, picking up her phone. I say nothing as I sit back on the sofa.

I'm about to drink some wine when I'm greeted by muffled moans coming from next door. I scrunch my nose and try not to block out the noises.

"What about these photos?" she suggests, holding her phone

to the camera.

"Aren't they a little... unprofessional?" I ask, not really enjoying the idea that a dozen men would be looking at my casual photos. I wasn't sure why, but it seems so intimate—a real insight into my life.

"Yeah, so? A dating profile isn't a job application, or an important letter to the CEO of Amazon. You can be cute, *and* show the fun side to you," she says, chuckling at my expense. "Okay, I've uploaded some of the photos I think will get you matches, and I've even written your bio," she says.

"Oh, God. Show me," I insist, drinking some more wine to soften this embarrassing blow. She clicks a few buttons and a *ping* sounds from my phone. I click on the link she sends me.

As I look through my profile, I realise I don't hate it, but I don't love it either.

"It's not as bad as I thought it was going to be. I'm confident about myself, but I'm not confident about putting myself out there and dating." I continue scrolling through the profile.

"Everything seems scary the first time. But you can do it." She smiles from ear to ear, showing her vote of confidence.

"Let's make it live," I say, daringly, clicking the "Publish" button.

"I suggest you download the app to your phone. It makes it a lot easier to swipe and to chat," she says. I waste no time in downloading the app, scared that if I don't do it now, I'll never do it.

We talk for another hour before I instruct her to end our call and make up with Sophia. Once she hangs up, I switch to the app on my phone. After watching the master at work, I feel like I have a pretty good idea of how to work all of this. Left for "No, thanks," right for "Hell yes."

How hard can it be?

On my phone, swiping starts to feel like a game to me—it doesn't seem real, so I fall into the trap of thinking I have nothing to worry about.

I look through a few more profiles, before moving from the sofa to make myself some hot chocolate. My backside is barely an inch off the sofa before I hear a *ping* indicating a match. My heart races and it no longer feels like a game—I have my first match and it all gets a little too real.

Slowly, I edge back to the sofa, pick up my phone and open up the notification.

Brandon, twenty-nine, not married, has no kids. Looking for a good time, not a long time.

I don't waste any time in clearing the notification off the screen because even though I have never been in the game, I know a massive player when I see one. Once you reach their DMs, it's a promised broken heart and months of expensive therapy. Even though I can afford that therapy, I know better than to waste my time on wannabe Leonardo DiCaprio.

Getting back up to return to the plan of making my hot chocolate, another *ping* sounds from my phone. I laugh, deciding to stick with the wine as I sit back on the sofa, and open up the notification. It's strangely addictive when you start to get matches, I feel like I'm back to my online shopping— without having to spend any money.

He has a very memorable face. His long brown hair, which falls just above his eyebrows, has a slight curl to it and his eyes are a bright blue. His smile is bright and big, looking happy in every photo, and I have no idea what I can say to him.

I sit there, looking at his profile, trying not to delete the app because of my nerves. I mean, what does one say in this situation?

"Hey, what's up?"

"What did you have for dinner?"

No, they're so incredibly boring. *I* wouldn't date me if I received those messages.

I press down on the app and hold my finger there until the big cross flashes, asking if I want to delete the app. I stare at it for the longest time before my eyes glance at the takeaway menu and the wedding invitation sitting side-by-side. I can almost hear the comments and questions at each wedding I've ever attended. This is enough for me to decide against deleting the app. I go back to the messages.

"Come on, *think*," I say to myself. I'm in marketing, for God's sake. I can literally sell anything to anyone, so why is this so difficult? Shaking my head and cracking my fingers, I set out on a mission.

I open Google and search, "Smooth pick-up lines." Scrolling through one of the articles I find, I can't help but cringe at some of these pick-up lines. Surprisingly, the least cringe line in the entire list has got to be, *"I hope you know CPR, because you just took my breath away."*

Thinking it's good enough ... *I think* ... I type the message. I feel like I'm about to jump out of a plane or walk out onto a train track. The adrenaline coursing through me is enough to power a Boeing 747.

Okay, here goes nothing.

I press "Send" and, as soon as I see the message has been delivered, I throw my phone down onto the sofa, shielding my eyes with my hand so I can't see what I've just done. I know deep down it's pointless, but it makes me feel better. I sit there for a few minutes, hoping and praying I haven't just embarrassed myself.

Ping.

My stomach flips as my mind races through all the bad possibilities of rejection and humiliation this message could entail.

1. *He's changed his mind, and he's no longer interested after closer inspection of my pictures.*
2. *He's pointed out all the flaws he can see within my pictures.*
3. *He's assumed I'm DTF, though he'll soon find out he's sorely mistaken.*
4. *He thinks it's sad that a twenty-nine-year-old is still single.*

I slowly uncover my eyes, peeking at the message waiting for me. But as I slowly read its contents, I'm surprised and slowly opened my second eye.

Aaron_Jones: *I'm a lawyer, so I don't know CPR, but I'll gladly try for you.*

I smile, my head tingling and my heart bursting as I read one of the most romantic things any guy has ever said to me. Which, in hindsight, speaks volumes for my love life.

Biting my lip, I think of another message to send back.

Rosiexx: *Well, if I have a case of medical negligence, I'm sure you'd be more than happy to oblige.*

Before I can overthink it, I send the message. My insides feel as though they are clenching as I think about what I'm doing. A few hours ago, I wouldn't have agreed to this.

Ping.

Aaron_Jones: *I'll do more than oblige. I've always wanted to become a Judge, so what do you think of my gavel?*

I frown, unsure of what he's trying to say. Before I can finish my message, asking what he meant, I'm sent an image. An image I wish I didn't see.

Gasping in disgust, I turn off my phone and shove it under the nearest cushion, trying to get that *thing* far away from me. I blink erratically—trying to erase that memory, but each time I blink, I can see it even more clearly.

I shiver in horror, and decide I've had enough of this app for one night—maybe forever.

Sighing, I get up from the sofa, dragging my velvet, navy blanket and wrapping it around my shoulders. As my phone remains buried deep beneath the cushions, I see the light shining from my laptop. I sigh, leaving my laptop logged in overnight and waking up to a dead battery is becoming a bad habit—so is leaving too many tabs open at once.

Maybe I should add these to the list of things I need to change before I turn thirty.

I begin to close each tab one by one. *Why are there so many?*

In my tired state, I must have forgotten that I'm still logged into my dating profile. Squealing again, I shut the laptop's lid and shiver at the awful, unwarranted sight.

I think I've been traumatised enough for one night.

I head off to bed, not sure if my eyes are burning from tiredness, or from that image.

I think my younger self was right—I don't think I'm cut out for this dating crap.

Chapter Two

It's been two days since I signed up for a dating app and I haven't glanced at my laptop since the unsolicited dick pic.

Now it's Monday and I need it for work but I can't bring myself to open the dirty thing. Instead, I take it to my friend Elijah's cafe. He can sort this out for me since his cafe is on the way to my office.

"Hey, Rosie!" Elijah exclaims, wiping his hands on his apron.

"You've got to help me," I say, holding out my laptop.

Frowning, he takes the laptop from my hands and holds it far away from his face as if it's an explosive bomb. "It's not going to burst into flames like your last one, right?" he asks, blowing on the back.

Laughing, I punch his arm and gently push him into the back, where no customer can be put through the same misery I have been subjected to.

"No, it won't explode, but there's something on there I don't wish to see…" I keep it vague, embarrassed to even say the words.

"What's so terrible you don't want to open up your laptop?" he asks, placing the laptop on a side table and crossing his arms, inquisitively. I bite my fingernails, cringing from the inside out.

"Just look." I want it gone.

He mutters an, "Okay" and opens the laptop.

"What's your password?"

"Sunflower, capital S."

"Cute."

He types in the password and is about to hit, "Enter," when I stop him.

"Wait!" I yelp. He pauses, flicking his eyes to mine, waiting for me to speak, "Turn it away from me ... I really don't want to go through that again."

Now he looks scared. His eyes are wide, and his mouth is pulled into a thin line. He turns the laptop so I can no longer see the screen, and looks back up to me.

"This isn't illegal, right? Because I don't want to go to jail. I'm not cut out for it, and I'm better than that," he whispers, looking behind him.

"No! It's just not something I want to see, that's all," I say, rubbing my arms.

"Well at least give me a hint."

I sigh, feeling my cheeks burn. "*You* have one."

"I have many, many things, Rosie. Be more specific." He tries to hide a smirk, and I begin to suspect he knows what I'm saying.

I lightly smack his arm. "You know what I mean!"

He wipes the smile from his face, suddenly serious. "I don't! Enlighten me." He crosses his arms.

"*A penis,*" I whisper, the word sounding alien on my tongue. Elijah bursts out laughing. I wait for him to stop, rolling my eyes and wishing I could disappear. The humiliation. *God*.

"Oh god, I bet you didn't like that!" he says, coughing as his laughter intensifies. He wipes a tear from his eyes, still wheezing.

"No, I didn't! I didn't ask for it, so why would I want to see … *that*?"

"Oh, that has made my day." He rubs his face with one hand, his laughter finally dying down. "Okay, let's sort this out for you."

He opens the laptop and clicks a few buttons before he shuts the laptop and returns it to me.

"You didn't even make a face or react in any way," I say, glad that my laptop is no longer tainted. "How are you so okay with seeing someone else's *thing*?"

"Thing? It's a penis, and I've seen a lot worse." He pauses, looking off into the distance and cringing. "*A lot worse.*"

"Anyway, how have you been?" I ask, deciding not to ask further questions on his suggestive statement.

"Somewhere between, on the verge of a breakdown, and absolutely fantastic!" I laugh. Knowing him, he's being one hundred percent honest.

"What about you? Besides your penis problem," he says, heading back into the cafe.

I roll my eyes. "I'm trying to meet a man," I answer, sitting on a bench near the till. His eyes raise to meet mine as he wipes the table.

"You? You're dating?" he asks, not even trying to hide his shock and disbelief.

"Yes, why is it so hard to believe?" I shove a nut in my mouth, only remembering how many dirty fingers must have touched this one nut prior. I spit it out on a napkin, ignoring Elijah's scoff.

"*The* Rosie? The Rosie who thinks she's cursed with all men? The Rosie who turns every guy down?"

My head lowers under his gaze.

"Yes! I spend my Friday nights alone, in my pyjamas with dinner for one," I answer, throwing my hands up in the air.

"*And*?" he asks, giving me a knowing smile.

I crinkle my nose, annoyed he can read me so well. "And my cousin is getting married, and I need a date for the wedding." I pick up another nut but then I immediately throw it back in the bowl. "Oh my God, please take these away from me!"

Elijah removes the bowl of tainted nuts and raises his eyebrows at me.

"You can't just send away nuts because some people may have touched them." His voice is suggestive, and I know what he's trying to say.

I throw him a sarcastic smile. "Is that seriously the best you can do?" He shrugs, shooting me a sly smirk and shaking the bowl of nuts. "I just want to meet someone nice, you know? Someone I can share my nights with. Someone I can share my life with." I rest my face in my hands, fed up with being alone.

"Well, you're already on dating sites. They're the way to go," he suggests, washing a glass and leaning against the counter.

"I've tried, but you've seen what I've been sent," I say, sighing.

"Rosie, you can't give up because you've seen *one* penis." I can tell he's trying not to laugh as he says that. "Trust me, I've had my fair share. Just brush it off and try again."

I consider it, but I'm incredibly unsure.

What if I've already met "the one" but blew it somehow?

And why can't we meet someone the old-fashioned way any more? It's all swiping left and right and putting so many filters on your pictures that you become an entirely different person. What happened to romance?

"I'll tell you what, I'll help you. I'll give you my dating expertise for free. But we are not doing it on your laptop. Hand me your phone," Elijah says, holding out his hand. I reluctantly place it in his hand without complaint, already exhausted with this whole dating thing.

He pulls a face as he goes through my phone. I don't think to ask until he begins to laugh.

"What? What is it?" I get up, trying to see what he can see. He moves the phone away from me.

"Trust me, you don't want to see that again." And I realise that he's talking about that photo.

Once the photo has been dealt with, Elijah flicks through some profiles, pulling faces and making sounds as he reads their bio and flicks through their photos. As he does this for a few minutes, serving customers occasionally, I think about the time we first met. We were in secondary school and Elijah was new. Within the first week, everyone found out that the two men bringing Elijah to school were *both* his dads. They would make fun of him, and everyone refused to let him hang out. I saw he was upset, and I went over and spoke to him. Ever since that day, we've been inseparable. I trust him with my life.

Eventually, he looks at me, eyes wide.

"I've found one," he says, turning the phone around so I can see.

"Can you not say it like that, please? Sounds like we're looking through a menu of our potential murder victims,"

I say.

"Was that not the assignment?" he asks, sarcasm lacing his words.

I say nothing, just stick my tongue out and gesture for him to continue.

"This guy's name is Michael, he's twenty-seven, and enjoys playing pool," he says, nodding his head in approval. I scrunch my nose—his smile drops and his eyes roll. "What's wrong with him?" He already knows the answer.

"I didn't think I'd date a "Michael" that's all," I say, trying to find reasons why it would be a very bad idea for me and him to date. I understand it makes me sound shallow, but in all my years of being single, I've built up the perfect man in my mind. I'm so nervous that the guy at least has to be perfect for me to imagine having any chance at happiness.

He sighs, turning the phone away from me and continuing with his search.

"You know, you're hard work."

"But I'm worth it."

"You better hope so or you'll be drinking terrible tasting red wine and dancing alone at Maddy's wedding in your *thirties*," he says, knowing how to push my buttons. There is nothing wrong with being single and thirty. I *know* that. I just want to finally have someone to share my life with.

"Fine, show me Michael again," I huff.

He turns my phone around again, showing me his profile.

"I guess he's not bad." I scrunch my nose again. "But I really don't like men who share their Snapchat—" I start to say before Elijah's extremely loud sigh stops me in my tracks. "Fine, I'll stay optimistic. I'm trusting you with this."

"When have I ever let you down?" he asks, shooting me his

arrogant, knowing smile.

"Arrogance doesn't suit you," I reply, gently tapping his arm.

"You're dating this guy, end of story. I'm going to message him now." He pauses, typing something. "And you'll thank me for it."

I let him do it, knowing I need to be pushed because my nerves will only get in the way. I'm interested to see how this goes.

My phone pings.

"Ah! Are you free tonight at seven? Of course, you are!" he says, not giving me a chance to answer as he types something, and presses send.

"You're now on for seven tonight. Make sure you don't show up wearing a suit and with your hair up," he says, handing me back my phone. I huff, never understanding how he can be so chill about dating. I seriously need to take a page out of his book.

"God, I feel like your fairy Godmother."

"Mother?" I arch my eyebrows, smirking. He flips me off as a customer stands by the till.

Elijah flashes them his best smile, pretending like he didn't just display utter profanities at me. I can't believe his charm.

I steal a glance at the customer and my heart jumps—it's Lucas.

"Can I grab a hot chocolate please, mate?" he asks, tapping his credit card on the table. Under my gaze, his penetrating brown eyes fall on mine, and he flashes a signature, dazzling smile.

"Hey," Lucas says, turning his body towards me. I can see Elijah watching this exchange with enjoyment as he makes Lucas his drink.

"Hi," I reply awkwardly, not sure what else I can say—I mean, we hardly know each other. It's funny, we've been living next door to each other for a few years, but we've barely shared three words, except when I give him his parcel, which sometimes finds its way into my mail.

"I'm Lucas," he says, outstretching his hand as if he's introducing himself.

Wait.

He *is* introducing himself. He has no idea who I am.

He's unbelievable. I think this beats what he said to his friends all those years ago. I've been his neighbour for years, and he doesn't even recognise me. Doesn't he remember what he said outside my front door?

I straighten in my chair, smirking at his outstretched hand, not attempting to reach for it. His eyes dip and he slowly retracts his hand.

"Elijah, I'll call you tonight with an update," I say, keeping eye contact with Lucas and speaking up so Elijah can hear me over the coffee machine as he continues to make Lucas's drink.

"No problem, see you later, Cinderella!" he says back, winking.

I get up from my chair, put my phone in my pocket and grab my laptop. I simply walk past him, not looking back, and the enjoyment of teasing Lucas begins to fade—being replaced by the stress over the fact I'm going on my very first date tonight. And I could not be less prepared.

Chapter Three

Upon entering my office, I immediately sink into my chair and log onto my laptop, no longer scared of what I may find there.

Sitting at my desk, surrounded by my notes and mood boards for my upcoming projects, I soon forget about the wedding and my quest for love. I feel at home here which, I know, some may find strange. Most people can't wait to leave the office, but when I'm home, I feel lonely and out of sorts. When I'm here, I feel productive and happy.

I check my calendar and I'm enthused to find that my first meeting is with one of my favourite clients, Rachel. Rachel is an author I've worked with since the beginning of her writing career, and I'm proud to say I've helped get her on three bestseller lists and a dozen on-screen interviews.

She's also one of my closest friends.

Before I check my emails or do absolutely anything at all, my intercom rings.

"Rosie, can you come into the conference room, please?"

Dylan—my boss—asks.

I quickly finish the article and gather my notes before heading into Dylan's office.

I enter the room, glad to see he's alone.

"I have a meeting with a client in about half an hour," I inform him.

"Take a seat, Rosie," he says, typing something up on his computer like he didn't just hear me.

I take a seat, holding my head up high.

He continues typing until the pressure is almost unimaginable.

Is he doing this on purpose? Is he trying to make me squirm?

Finally, he swivels his chair towards me and gives me the, *"You know what I'm about to say"* smile.

Do I?

"I've been looking at your data and client numbers, and they're down from previous years. In fact, they're the lowest I've ever seen from you," he says, grabbing a file from his bottom drawer.

"I've just not had a good month, that's all," I try to explain, not really wanting to talk about my personal life.

He places a piece of paper on the table in front of me. I don't lean forward, but I drop my eyes, reading it from afar. Dylan says nothing as I read the paper in front of me.

"I don't understand," I say, picking up the paper and thinking I must have misread something.

"We are going to be posting a new position soon. It's for the Chief of Marketing—my job, and I want to offer you a promotion," he says after a moment of silence and confusion that fills the room up like icy water.

"But you said my numbers are down. Doesn't that usually

have the *opposite* effect?" *Stop talking, Rosie, and accept the promotion! This is what we've been working towards!*

"That's the thing…" He leans forward in his white swivel chair, and I realise that this is not going to be so simple—with Dylan, there is always a catch. "I *can't* offer it to you until I see a *big* change. There are other people in this office who are surpassing your numbers, and HR wants me to extend the job offer to whomever I think is capable—whether that means we do an internal promotion, or hire externally."

My heart stops. I can taste a coppery substance sitting on my tongue, making it hard to swallow.

I can't believe I'm having to compete with other people in the office. I'm the Lead Marketer.

"But surely the Lead Marketer should be the next Chief Marketer?" I ask, flustered and trying my best to see why he's doing this.

I can't take seeing someone else walking around with that promotional title—*my* promotional title—on their ID badge.

"We have to be fair and let everyone apply. I'm just giving you a heads up that I want you, but you need to convince HR that you're capable, by upping your numbers," he states, taking a sip of his coffee. I sit there, imagining the coffee slipping from his fingers and spilling the hot liquid all over his perfect, white, cotton shirt.

"So, let me get this straight"—I sit forward in my chair— "you're not offering me the position?" He shakes his head, still smiling like the Cheshire Cat.

"I need to see your improvement before I can."

I get up from my chair, feeling deflated.

I want and *need* this promotion.

Before I leave, I turn around to look at Dylan. "Why are you leaving, if you don't mind me asking?"

Dylan scratches his chin. "I've been offered a position as the Vice President of this company. It doesn't start until August, so you have time before I have to make a decision."

"Congratulations, that's great news," I say, feeling the tiniest shred of envy.

Dylan presses the intercom button, the moment I've left the chair, "Sadie, can you come in, please?"

I leave the room, and of course, bump into the Wicked Witch herself. Sadie is the new Junior Marketer who has been trying to poach my client, Rachel. I grind my teeth, unsure if I'm dreaming—if I am, it's a nightmare. Surely she can't apply for the job of Chief Marketer? That job needs a lot more experience than a few weeks of average work.

Sadie oozes a venomous aura that seems to repel anyone who crosses her path, besides Dylan, apparently. Her black hair, which resembles deadly poison, serves as a perfect match to her soulless, cold eyes that glint with a calculating and cunning nature. With a sly smirk plastered on her thin, deceitful lips, she takes pleasure in playing manipulative mind games to get ahead in her career, even if it means stepping on others without remorse. Her appearance lacks any hint of charm or grace, as her personality leaks out of every pore.

Sadie's approach to success is fuelled by her merciless ambition. She doesn't hesitate to backstab or betray colleagues and acquaintances to climb the ladder of success, leaving a trail of broken relationships and crushed spirits in her wake. Usually, I'd praise and applaud an ambitious woman, but Sadie is different. With her insatiable thirst for power and success, she is willing to sacrifice any sense of morality to get what she wants. Friends are merely stepping-stones, and loyalty is a foreign concept to her. Despite her young age, Sadie's soul is already tainted, making her a cautionary tale of what ambition—unchecked—can lead to. I can't let her take this promotion, or else we're all doomed.

I scoff at the sight of her grey, oversized blazer and belt. I just don't understand why that's now considered "fashion." Her round glasses are sitting on top of her black fringe, magnifying her judging eyes.

"Rosie," she addresses me with heavy disdain.

I don't acknowledge her. Usually, I'm a lot more polite and professional. But today? I couldn't care less.

It's war.

I continue walking to my office, relieved to see Rachel sitting outside. She gets up once she sees me but her smile fades at the sight of the anger swirling around me like a tornado.

"What's happened?" she asks. I say nothing, barrelling into my office with her on my fiery tail. Once the door is shut, I practically word vomit about what just happened. Rachel listens, her face getting redder and redder with anger with each word I spew.

"Are you joking? You've done everything for this job in the last five years. I can't believe that man's *audacity*," she says in her classic, Rachel sassiness, clicking her fingers and tutting.

"Well, he was trying to warn me about my numbers so I stand more of a chance," I say, indignant, but also pleased that she sees my side so clearly.

Rachel shakes her head and makes noises of disdain. "Yeah, but he's also telling everyone else in the office about the promotion and that they should up their numbers. If you ask me, he isn't giving you a chance, he's making it a competition so the company can profit before he's Vice President!" she exclaims, her eyes as wide as saucers.

I sag in my chair, wishing I could ease the gnawing feeling in my stomach.

"Nope, sit up," Rachel demands, marching towards me. She pulls my chair out from under my desk and attempts to make me sit up straight.

"Why? I'm sad. I might as well be comfortable."

"We are going to come up with an idea to help you win. I don't need you sulking right now," she says, grabbing my board pen. She heads over to the whiteboard and writes:

Million-Pound Idea to get Rosie that Damn Promotion.

"Okay, I guess I can entertain this."

"That's what I like to hear," she praises.

"Okay, so you need a success story, right?" she asks. I nod, still feeling like the room is closing in on me.

"Helllooo?" Rachel asks, waving the pen in my face. I blink. "Sorry."

"Come on, help me think of an idea!" she says, pointing to the board.

We sit in my office for almost half an hour, coming up with a grand total of three ideas. All of which have no legs to stand on.

"Maybe I am out of my depth here, Rachel," I say, throwing my hands in the air, worried that I am in fact too old for this market.

"No, you're not out of it. You have literally made my dreams come true. I wake up and I'm on a new bestsellers list, and I have emails from celebrities. My books are literally reaching new countries in hundreds of different languages! That's all because of you," she says, sitting on the chair in front of me. "You've helped me all of these years, and I'm going to help you."

Her vow makes me feel a tiny shred of hope and, to my surprise, it sparks an idea. I sit up and search for something on my computer.

"Girl, I love that look on your face!" Rachel says, smiling. "You have a cool idea; I just know it."

I look up the numbers for Rachel's orders and my suspicions are correct—her numbers are declining since the last book launch. She wrote a romance book called, *Sweeter than Sugar*, and it was a massive success. But we haven't had a launch in over six months, and things are starting to go quiet.

"Your numbers are down since the last launch," I say, showing her the computer screen.

She looks at me, confusion swirling in her blue eyes. "Thanks for that. Why are you kicking me when *you're* the one down?" she asks, rolling her eyes.

"No, don't you understand? Your numbers are down, so *my* numbers are down. We've become too comfortable, and that's exactly why I'm losing. We need to get out of this comfort."

Rachel frowns, the cogs in her mind working overtime. "So, we need to think of another book idea?"

"Exactly. You can be the client," I say. "If we pull off a huge promotion, with serious results, I might have a chance at winning" I exclaim. If I know anything about myself, it's that I can market just about anything.

"We can help each other," she says, the excitement in the room sizzling at an all-time high.

I check the time. We have about half an hour left of the meeting before I'm with another client.

"*Sweeter than Sugar* was released in April, we both know you need to write another book," I say, standing and going over to the board.

"In the meantime, I can sort out the marketing campaign here and we can make it bigger than last time." I draw a graph and timeline to show Rachel the facts.

"But I don't have an idea for a book which is remotely ready to publish."

"Okay, so we need to brainstorm book ideas," I say, knowing I'm going above and beyond this time; I have to.

"Perhaps you can come back tomorrow, and we can get to work?" I say, wrapping the meeting up as I glance at the clock again.

"Are you free tonight?" she asks, gathering her things and placing them in her bag. "I really want to make this a priority."

I have a date tonight.

But ... *This* is now my priority.

"Okay, I'll cancel my date. You want to come over to my place around eight?" I ask, slightly relieved that I no longer have to embarrass myself in front of anyone tonight.

"Wait, what? Back up," she says, dropping her bag on the table.

"What?" I ask.

"A date? *You*? You're going on a date?"

"Okay, try and hide some of your disbelief," I say, rolling my eyes.

"Don't cancel it! We'll meet tomorrow. You need to get laid."

"Excuse me? I'm perfectly fine!" I assure in a high-pitched tone, already feeling my cheeks burning up.

"Rachel, when was the last time you got laid? By an actual man?" she asks. I wasn't in the mood to say a big, fat grand total of zero men have ever got me laid, so I go with the alternative.

"It has been a while, but I'm fine with that. I don't need a man, I need that promotion," I say, hoping Rachel will drop this subject. It's not something I like to talk about. It's not like I've never had the chance to be with a man, it's just I never really wanted to. My job has always been first, and a man will just get in the way. Just like my father did with my mother. He spent years wasting her time while he climbed the job market, got her pregnant and then left her with nothing. He cheated on her and that was that.

That's not going to be me.

"Rosie, go on the date. We can meet tomorrow," she insists.

"Really, I don't want to. I need this promotion, you under-stand that."

"If you say so," she says, pursing her lips.

As Rachel is about to leave, the image of the gold invitation letter, which is sitting on my dining room table, hits me. I need a date to the wedding, or else I'll always be known as the woman who never has a date. I'll become the old aunty who gets drunk at every party and hits on the barmen to try and get discounted drinks.

"Okay, okay, I'm sorry but I can't meet tonight. I shouldn't? Should I? No, I need to go on that date because I have a bloody wedding later this year," I say, really starting to hate today.

As I say this, Rachel's eyes flash with excitement.

"What?" I ask, really hoping it isn't about my sex life.

"What if my book is about your life?" she asks, tugging a brown strand behind her ear, deep in thought.

"Huh?"

"Just picture it. Successful woman goes on a series of dates, trying to find 'the one' for a wedding"—she pauses, then gasps—"before she turns thirty!" she exclaims, clapping her hands at the thought.

"I don't know, Rach…" I say, not entirely thrilled about this idea.

"What? Come on, it'll help us both. We can keep a diary of the dates you go on and of course, embellish the details for added drama and effect."

"I don't want my life shown to millions of people. I might as well kiss that promotion goodbye! As well as my love life." I sigh.

"We can make it anonymous. We can change the name, say it's a work of fiction and voila! Why else do you think people love my novels?" She pauses, but doesn't let me answer. "Because I write about real people, with relatable problems!"

I stare at her, my heart thudding and yet … I can't believe I'm considering this. Am I really this desperate?

Yes. Apparently, I am that desperate.

"As long as it's not obvious it's me." I sigh. "And as long as we really embellish the details."

Rachel makes a noise which reminds me of the sound a teenage girl makes when they just find out they just made Prom Queen.

"This is going to work!" she declares.

Will it?

Chapter Four

"He literally just texted you, saying you have to meet him at the restaurant. He's not even going to come and pick you up?" Madilyn complains over the phone as I'm finishing off my hair.

"Yeah, well it's the twenty-first century. I guess he thinks he's being polite and giving me my independence," I say, trying to give him the benefit of the doubt. Dating in these times is already confusing enough—throw the need for equality in there, and chivalry is basically a goner.

"Yeah, but he can still pick you up. What's next? Not going to open the door for you?" she asks, huffing and puffing over the phone. I laugh, putting the final finishes on my hair, finally happy with it.

"Honestly, I think I prefer meeting him there. That way he doesn't have my address," I reason. She's quiet for a moment before she sighs like she wants to say more but thought better of it. I guess we'll just have to agree to disagree.

"Anyway, I've got to go, so wish me luck," I say, grabbing my bag and jacket.

"Good luck. Just keep me updated, and if you need a 9-9-9 emergency, I've got your back," she whispers.

Laughing, I say my goodbyes and set out on my journey for love. As I think that, I almost gag and most definitely cringe. I've always wanted love, but it has never been in the cards for me. I would have crushes on boys from school, but I was always the last choice. Sometimes I was the second choice, but that always felt even more insulting. It was like I was so close to something I wanted but could never quite grasp it. At least if I was a sixth, seventh, or eight choice, I had no hope to grasp onto so it was easier to forget.

I step on the crisp, dry leaves, enjoying the cold, refreshing air on my cheeks. It's dark outside, but the overhead orange street lights illuminate my path. When I was younger, I used to imagine the street lights were stars—shining on your path, so you're never lost and blind on your travels. They were the closest I could get to stars, and I would make wishes and ask questions about why I was alone and where my person was. Thinking back to it now, it seems sad. I was always fascinated by astronomy, and somewhere along my life, I just stopped.

Maybe I stopped when the wishes never came true.

I open the door to the restaurant, and I'm greeted by a pleasant jingle of bells above me.

He said he was going to be wearing jeans and a red shirt. I like the fact he's wearing a red shirt because red is the colour of love, after all. I imagine he's wearing satin which flows as he walks.

"May I help you?" The waiter asks, giving me a dry smile.

"I have a reservation with Michael?" I say, scanning the room. I think I remember what he looks like from his photos, but I can't be sure. People always look different in real life. I just hope he isn't sixty years old with high blood pressure.

"If you would like to follow me," the waiter instructs, grabbing a menu. My heart starts racing as my self-destructing brain reminds me this is my first ever date. As the waiter leads me down the row of tables with couples laughing and holding hands, planning their future together, I'm trying not to be sick at the thought of small talk and pleasantries.

You've got this, Rosie, I think to myself, taking slow deep breaths. *Just think of this as a business meeting.*

"Here we are," the waiter says, stopping at a table and pulling my chair out.

I look up to see Michael stand from his chair and hold his hand out. I place mine in his, hoping it's not too sweaty from my nervous breakdown.

"You must be Rosie," he says, shaking my hand. It isn't a bad handshake. In fact, it's firm yet gentle. If that's any indicator on Michael, then I'm in good hands.

"Yes, and you must be Michael," I say, sitting down and taking the menu from the waiter.

"I hope so, or else this would be an awful mix up!" he jokes, chuckling to himself and taking a sip of water.

"I hope you haven't been waiting too long," I say, reading the choices on the menu.

"It's fine, we can't *all* be punctual," he says, his voice sarcastic. My eyes flick to his, hearing the slight dig in that comment. We said we would meet at seven and it's only ten past seven.

I force a chuckle as the uncomfortable feeling in my stomach comes back. I continue to look at the menu, really focusing on the options. Michael seems nice enough—his blond, curly hair makes him look like a surfer out in Australia and I can almost smell the salty waves. His face is sharp with freckles dotted over the bridge of his nose which I find endearing. You can't really see those from his pictures, but they frame his face in real life. As my eyes continue their sneaky perusal, I notice something I should have noticed the moment we sat down.

He's wearing a football shirt. A *red* football shirt.

He notices me looking and grabs the badge sitting on his chest.

"I've supported this team from the moment I came out of my mother's vagina. This shirt is my lady magnet and good luck charm," he boasts it as if the news is impressive. I find it slightly repulsive.

"Oh, that's nice," I say, resisting the urge to see how far I am away from an exit point.

"Yeah, I've had every new shirt for the past twenty-seven years. This shirt was bought for me by my ex-girlfriend," he says, his smile fading. He sits back in the chair as if he's said something which upset him.

"Are you okay?" I ask, not sure if I want to even ask that question.

He sighs and takes another sip of his water.

"It's just I'm not totally over my ex. She was my soulmate and best friend," he says, his eyes becoming hooded.

Oh. *Oh.*

I can't believe this is my first date. *Is life trying to screw with me?*

"I see," I say, unsure of what I can do. I didn't want to leave because I feel like that is incredibly rude, but at the same time, this date isn't even ten minutes in and I'm in physical pain—actual bodily pain. "I'm sorry about that. Have you chosen what you want to order?" I ask, thinking if I divert the conversation back to safe dating questions, maybe we can salvage the next hour.

He looks at the menu with his hooded eyes and clears his throat. His eyes browse the selection of food, and I hope that's the end of the most awkward conversation I think I've ever had.

He places the menu down and rests his head in his hands. I roll my eyes and massage my forehead, already feeling a headache coming on.

"I'm sorry, it's just this is the same restaurant I took Amy to on our first date," he explains, his voice whiny and full of sadness and longing. Is he joking? Usually I'd feel sorry for him, but this situation is unprecedented.

"Look, if you're still in love with your ex, maybe we shouldn't be here?" I suggest grabbing my bag and getting ready to stand up.

He removes his face from his hands and gestures to me to sit back down. In an ideal world, I would be running, and I wouldn't look back. But in this world, I need a date to a wedding and a very important promotion. To get that promotion, I need to exploit my love life even if that means living a life of misery for a few months. My life depends on it.

I slowly sit back down, hating every second of it.

"I'm sorry, I won't go on about her. It's just very fresh and new and I'm struggling to deal with it," he explains. Hmm, maybe he isn't so bad. I've never had to deal with a breakup before, so who am I to say it's easy?

"It's okay," I say, not saying to him that I understand, because I really don't. Instead, I pick up my menu and choose the arrabbiata pasta with garlic bread.

"I think I've decided, what about you?" I ask, racking my

brain with conversational questions.

"I think I'll have the steak and ribs," he says. I nod, appreciating his choice and looking over at the waiter to let him know we've decided. He walks over, notepad in hand, and gestures for me to order first. I don't hesitate. The last thing I ate was some chicken salad at lunch. I'm starving.

"Can I please order the arrabbiata pasta with the garlic bread on the side?" I ask, pointing out my choice. The waiter nods and writes my order. My mouth waters at the thought of it.

"And for you?" he asks, looking at Michael. He has his head in his hands again, sniffling.

Oh God, please not now, I pray.

"He'll have the steak and ribs, please," I say quickly, trying to avoid another awkward encounter. But by the looks of the waiter, the encounter is already happening.

"Is he okay?" he asks, looking over at Michael with concern on his face.

"Yeah, we're just having a really deep conversation," I say, hoping the waiter leaves it at that. He doesn't, of course.

He frowns at me as if I've broken his heart and tuts as he puts his notepad in his pocket and walks away, shaking his head.

Oh great, I'm going to enjoy my spit arrabbiata. I watch as the waiter walks over to his waiter buddies and says something to them. They all react shocked and then their eyes snap to my table along with the rest of the restaurant.

"Michael, people are starting to stare," I say, fed up with this already. Why can't I go on a nice date, with a nice guy, and enjoy my bloody pasta!

"I'm sorry," he says, sniffling. He finally lifts his head from his hands, and I cringe at the sight of his red eyes and wet eye lashes. I'm mortified and cannot believe this is happening. I used to be obsessed with those cheesy, cringe television programmes where people would go on awful dates, and I always thought they were scripted or wouldn't happen to me. Well, now I feel stupid.

"So, what do you do for work?" I ask, hoping he won't try and bring this back to his ex.

"I'm a painter and decorator," he answers. *Oh god*, even his job is boring.

"You?" He sniffles.

"I'm a Marketing Executive," I say. I see his eyebrows rise and his eyes dry up.

"That's so interesting! Do you have a lot of clients?" he asks. I straighten my back, glad this date is finally taking shape into an actual adult conversation.

"I do have a lot of clients, but I adore my job. I'm working with an author right now," I say, incredibly proud of that fact. I'm not proud because she helps me bring in the big numbers. I'm proud because I take on clients who are respectable and put the work in.

"Wow! My ex loved books," he says.

That's it.

I stand up and grab my bag, no longer able to do this. I tried, but I failed.

"I'm sorry. That's the last thing I'll say about her!" he exclaims, his eyes begging for me to sit down.

"I'm sorry, but it's just not going to work out. Now, if you excuse me, I have a bottle of wine with my name on it," I say before giving him one last smile. "It was nice to meet you, Michael."

I walk out of the restaurant, leaving behind my delicious

pasta along with my pride. I pull my phone out and text Rachel.

Rosie: *Worst date I'll ever go on. In fact, I do not want to continue with this humiliation. We'll have to think of another idea tomorrow.*
Rachel is typing...
Rachel is typing...
Rachel: *Good. We don't have to embellish the details and we'll have our next best seller! We're doing this.*

I groan, wishing she just agreed with me.

I push my phone back into my bag.

After walking for what seems life forever, I decide to pop into my all-time favourite Greek, fast-food place for a Gyros wrap. Sitting in the brightly lit restaurant in my romantic, date outfit, alone ... I've never felt more stupid. I'm extremely independent, but I just don't know how I'm going to find a date for the wedding, help Rachel with her book, and snag the promotion. Everything seems so far away, and for the first time in my life, I want to give up.

"Hey," someone says behind me. I turn, still trying to chew and swallow the wrap I just shoved in my mouth.

It's Lucas.

I cover my mouth, trying to chew the food faster, but my throat dries up at the sight of him. He stands over my table smirking at my attempt.

"You good?" he asks, folding his arms over his chest. I have to really try not to look at the way his muscles strain against his shirt.

"I'm good," I say, not sure why he's speaking to me. I'm still unsure if he knows who I am.

"Rosie, isn't it?" he asks, pulling a chair out and sitting

down like I invited him. I didn't invite him, so I think this is incredibly rude. I could be with someone tonight.

"So, you figured it out?" I ask, taking a sip of my Coke, smirking.

"I'm sorry if I didn't recognise you at the café. We don't see each other a lot, and I don't have the best memory," he admits, scratching his chin.

"You often forget women's names and faces?" I ask, leaning forward and enjoying the shock in his eyes. He coughs and smirks like I've said something funny.

"I just don't have the best memory," he says again. I can't stop thinking about what he said to his friends so I'm having a hard time trusting his apology.

"Must be hard when you have so many appointments in the week. Maybe you should keep a calendar. Tuesday, Gabby, Wednesday, Bridget, and so on."

He laughs, amused by my attempt at sarcasm.

"You assume a lot about me, but you barely know me," he says. He doesn't seem offended, in fact, he seems intrigued and ever so curious.

"I can hear your Friday nights from my living room, bedroom, and bathroom. I think I know you just fine."

His eyebrows raise and he licks his lips, contemplating what he's going to say next. I keep eye contact, never once looking at his lips. I don't want to give him that impression. I'm not interested in his red, plump lips in the slightest.

"I apologise, but it's not my fault the walls are paper thin." He leans forward and lowers his voice, "I can hear through the wall as well," he says, insinuating something. I rack my brain, thinking about what he can possibly be suggesting. I guess I do watch the TV quite loudly, and maybe I like to sing while showering. But how is that the same as what I can hear? I search his face for the answers, and he grins.

Oh my god.

He doesn't mean? No.

Oh...My...God.

My face burns as the blood rushes to the surface at this utterly mortifying realisation. "Excuse me," I say, my voice clipped as I try to control my rage and try to get the blood to retreat from my face.

"Look, I think we've gotten off at the wrong foot. Can we start again?" he asks, holding out his hand.

I just look at it, folding my arms. He must be joking. First, he insults me outside my own door, then he doesn't remember I'm his neighbour, and now this? He's having a laugh.

"I'm waiting for someone, actually," I say, my voice still clipped. I just hope he believes me and leaves me alone.

He looks me up and down, assessing if my outfit is date material. I fold my arms across my chest tighter, feeling insecure as his eyes continue to roam. I clear my throat, stopping him in his tracks.

"So, where is he?" he asks, leaning back in his chair. His mouth slackens like he doesn't believe me.

"Coming," I say, feeling my cheeks blush again. His eyes fall to my food.

Shit.

"He wasn't hungry?" he asks, biting his lip to hide a smirk. This guy is a major jerk.

"Look, I just want to be alone. I've had a crap night, and I just can't be arsed for pointless conversation with the likes of you. So, if you'll excuse me, I'll take this to go." Lucas's smirk finally vanishes, and he holds his hands up.

"Whatever you say."

I huff, packing up my food and pushing my chair under the table with a thud. Lucas sits there, watching me as I pack away my things, my temper rising with every passing second.

"See you later," he says, and I continue to ignore him.

I walk out of the Greek place, my face still burning and my heart racing. As the cold air hits my flushed cheeks and the sound of roaring traffic and low chatter from couples and families making small talk, I make a mental note to be quieter in the evenings.

Chapter Five

"**H**ave you got any leads?" Dylan asks, sticking his head around my open office door.

"I do, as a matter of fact!" I revel, standing up and fetching my files with my beautiful graphs and even more stunning statistics.

He walks down the corridor of our office, and I follow behind him, trying to explain the plan Rachel and I have conjured up.

"Rachel needs another bestseller, right?" I ask, cursing my choice of footwear. I never usually wear heels, so why did I think it was a good idea *today*?

I try to keep up without breaking both of my ankles.

"Francesca, can you make me a copy of these marketing plans?" he asks, dropping a stack of paper on Fran's desk. Francesca is a receptionist at the firm, and Dylan's personal lap dog.

"Yes, boss!" she says, frantically, scrambling to get up from her desk and immediately sets off towards the printer, dropping a few sheets as she goes. I roll my eyes but keep them stuck on the prize.

"Dylan, did you hear me?" I ask, feeling the sweat start to form as I struggle to keep up with him.

"What?" he asks, picking up another folder and scanning the contents.

"Rachel? She needs a bestseller, right?" I repeat, wishing he'd slow down.

"Yes, of course I do. We're behind on her next launch."

"Exactly. Rachel and I have decided to do a little research into online dating and show the tragic and awful dates people endure, just for love. We thought she could write a book on it," I explain, crossing my fingers, hoping he likes the idea.

"Okay, why do you think that is a bestselling idea?"

Excellent question.

"I've researched the market, and these tropes and themes are in right now. The online dating scene is trending because it's relatable, and it's now the number one way people meet. On top of that, dating in general is trending on all major search engines," I say, still following behind him.

His eyebrow cocks. "Hmm," he ponders, slowing down a touch. "So will this be fiction?"

"It'll follow the same rules and principles of a Romantic Comedy. It'll be light-hearted, funny, and awfully tragic."

"I love it. I want you two to get started right away," he instructs. He turns his head and reveals an excited smile and his eyes flash with pound signs. "Don't let me down." And with that, he speeds up and I stop. In some ways, I'm excited to be working with Rachel on a project again, but I don't think I'm happy about using my love life as inspiration for a book.

As I slink back into my office, and start planning the

marketing strategy for the novel, I hear a *ping* come from my phone.

Shutting my eyes, I reach into my back pocket whilst trying to simultaneously keep the folders and files from falling onto the floor.

I check my notifications, hoping it's something good. I need something good. It's from that cringe, immature dating site.

Gabe: *Hey, do you want to hear a joke about ghosts?*

That's weird. I really don't want to hear a joke about ghosts, but I'll bite.

I click on the notification, wanting to check out his profile. His name is Gabe, and he's twenty- nine. He's a journalist, and likes to spend his time outdoors. He's, thankfully, over six foot. I can't have a guy who is shorter than me because of my love for a heel. It just cannot happen.

Okay, even though I'm not one hundred percent sure I want to go back on a date, he seems interesting and nice enough.

Rosiexx: *Sure?*

I send the message and walk into my office, getting ready to call Rachel with some updates.

Ping.

I don't hesitate to read it.

Gabe: *That's the spirit!*

I can't help but laugh. I re-read the message at least five more times before I'm confident enough to reply.

Rosiexx: *That was ridiculously cheesy. How many women have you used that line on?*
   Gabe is typing...

I hold my breath, waiting for his response. Part of me wants to throw my phone away so I don't see what he says, and another part wants to stare at the phone until his message comes through. I feel like a teenager again, and I'm unsure as to why. Why does my heart start to race and my palms start to sweat when I'm talking to a man?

Gabe: *Have dinner with me tomorrow, and maybe I'll give you an answer.*

I bite my lip, hesitating. On one hand, I want and need to find someone. But, on the other hand, I don't think I can take another date like last night.

Before I can decide, my phone flashes with Rachel's gorgeous face.

I accept the call, thinking it's probably best if I give it a minute before I reply to Gabe.

"Spill the beans, girl!" Rachel screams. I remove the phone from my ear, cringing at the annoyingly high frequency.

"Damn, are you trying to hurt me?" I ask, rubbing my ear.

"Just spill the beans, and no one gets hurt!" she says.

Rolling my eyes, I decide it's in my ear's best interest to comply.

"There are no beans to spill. It was awful. Just awful. In fact, I'm not sure I can take another date like that again."

"What did he do?" she asks, not even trying to conceal her snicker.

"He wouldn't stop going on about his ex. Plus, he took me to *their* restaurant, and then cried in front of all the staff and customers. I was mortified, Rachel!"

I can hear Rachel's snicker growing over the phone. I can see how this is funny, but it isn't funny if you're the one watching a grown man cry and sob over an ex in the middle of a restaurant. I can never go to that place again, nor would I want to.

"Just get it out of your system." I sigh, placing her on speaker phone and sitting at my desk with my head in my hands.

"I'm sorry! But you just can't make this stuff up!" she says, still laughing at my expense.

"Well, you better write about it, because I'm doing this for you!" I say.

"And I'm doing this for you! We've got to help each other in this cut-throat world." She has a point, she *is* helping me. I need a date to the wedding, *and* that promotion. I can't get that promotion unless I knock last year's numbers out of the water. I can do that with Rachel's audience.

"Have you got another date planned?" she asks, finally settling down. I can hear scratching over the phone. I frown and try to ignore it.

"Actually, a guy named Gabe has asked me to dinner," I say, flicking back onto the messages between him and I.

"Okay! Have you accepted yet?" she asks, the scratching sound still in the background.

"I haven't yet, but I will."

"Well get on it! I need juicy stories!"

Scratch.

Scratch.

"Rachel, what's that noise?" I ask.

"I'm just writing some notes on the date. It would help if

you sent me a word document with some details, and I can get started on chapter three!"

Rachel and I talk for a few more minutes before I need to go into a meeting with a client. I send Gabe a quick message to tell him I'm interested in going out tomorrow, and to text me the time and location. I can't go out tonight because I have another date. Who would've thought I'd be booked out two evenings in a row?

We'll see what love has in-store for me.

***

I close my umbrella, shaking off the last droplets of the evening rain as I walk into my building. My footsteps echo on the marble floor, mingling with the distant hum of traffic outside. It has been a relentless day at work following an even more gruelling date—if you could even call it that. As I was walking out of the office, a man named Peter had messaged me on the app, asking if he could take me out to a restaurant tonight. Loneliness had gotten the best of me, compelling me to say yes. What that loneliness had actually done was sabotage me and find me a guy who spent the entire evening talking about his collection of antique spoons.

The elevator door opens and, as fate would have it, there stands Lucas. Our eyes meet for an awkward moment as I recall our rather intense conversation in the Greek place. Lucas manages to unstick his tongue from the roof of his mouth as he nods his head in greeting.

"Hey," he says.

"Hi," I reply, stepping into the small, box-like space.

We both look at the buttons, wondering who is going to press first. I reach out my hand searching for the button to the seventh floor, only to find his hand instead.

We pull back, almost simultaneously, as if burned by the contact.

"Sorry," I mumble, my cheeks flushing a subtle shade of pink.

"No, it's fine," he says, pressing the button for the seventh floor.

The elevator starts its ascent, the silence thickening between us like a heavy fog. I grip the handle of my bag, trying to think of something—*anything*—to say.

"Long day?" he asks, filling the silence.

"You have no idea." I sigh, thinking about the catalogue of spoons I had described to me in excruciating detail over dinner.

He chuckles but doesn't inquire further.

"Hey, I'm sorry if I offended you the other day. I was introducing myself because we haven't actually officially met. I always take your mail, but we've never spoken. I thought introducing myself would be polite," he explains, sheepishly.

I sigh, suddenly feeling awful by the way I reacted. "It's okay. I was having a bad day, so anyone could have set me off."

He nods, a small smile on his lips. We are wrapped once again in the awkward silence that so often seemed to define our interactions. My eyes dart to the numbers above the door, praying for the elevator to move faster.

"I had a date tonight," I blurt out, surprising myself.

"Oh?" He looks genuinely intrigued.

"Yeah, I downloaded that dating app everyone uses, and it's safe to say, the dating world sucks," I say, regretting every word that comes out of my mouth, but I can't stop it.

Lucas chuckles, nodding in agreement. "I hear that. I've been there. The world of online dating is a strange place. Why are you putting yourself through dating if you hate it so much?" he asks, generally curious.

I raise my eyebrows as if the answer is obvious. "Same reason everyone does it—I would like to date again. Especially because I'd like a date for my cousin's wedding." As I say it, I want to slap myself. *Why did I say that?*

Lucas scratches his chin. "If you need a date to the wedding, I'll happily help out," he suggests, looking a little sheepish.

I laugh like he's joking. I stop once I realise he isn't joking. "Are you being serious?"

He nods. "Yeah, I'd be happy to help."

I rub my arms, unsure of what to say. I'd appreciate it, but something feels weird to me as he's my neighbour. I don't want to humiliate myself, and have to live next to him…

"Thank you, but I should be okay," I say, feeling slightly awkward.

"Let me know if you do need help. How did the date go?" He says, swiftly moving the subject on, which I'm extremely happy about.

"Let's just say I'll never look at spoons the same way again."

Lucas laughs, a genuine sound that fills the small space between us. "That bad, huh?"

"Worse."

The elevator dinged, announcing our arrival on the seventh floor. As the door opens, we both head towards our flats. As we walk side by side in silence, Lucas finally breaks the silence. "So, how was work?"

"Same old, same old," I say, forcing another smile. "You?"

"Very busy with writing." He laughs. "I feel like I'm always busy."

"Yeah, I've noticed," I say before I can stop myself.

Lucas looks at me, puzzled. "Is that a good thing or a bad thing?"

I hesitate. This is my chance to bring up the years of loud music, the constant parade of women. But as I look into his eyes, I see a kindness and a softness I never noticed before.

"Let's just say it's hard not to notice you," I say, navigating each word like it's a step across a minefield.

The corners of Lucas's mouth twitch upwards, slowly blooming into a full-fledged grin. "I'll take that as a compliment."

I laugh nervously, pulling out my keys from my bag of chaos. Juggling my phone, an overstuffed wallet, and about four tubes of lip balm and tissues, I finally manage to unlock my door.

"See you around, Rosie," he says. I like the way he says my name, and I find myself smiling, momentarily forgetting about my crammed bag.

"Yeah, see you around," I reply, my voice tinged with a warmth that surprises even me.

Lucas freezes, his hand on his doorknob. "Oh, Rosie! Wait there." He ducks into his flat, and for a moment I'm left standing there, wondering why he needs me to wait here.

He emerges holding a parcel wrapped in brown paper, which doesn't reveal the contents. "This is yours. It came today," he says, smirking like he's privy to some cosmic joke.

My brow furrows. "That's weird, I haven't ordered anything. Thanks, anyway."

He hands me the parcel with a twinkle in his eye.

I retreat to the sanctuary of my flat, already puzzled about what's in the package. As I close the door, I hear him call, "Trust me, you'll love it!"

Curiosity bubbling over, I hastily cut through the brown parcel tape and pop open the box. My eyes widen as I see a sex toy nestled inside, along with a note that reads:

For when you're stressed. I haven't heard yours in a while, and I assumed it's broken. Thought this could help ;)

Staring at the contents, I burst into laughter. My eyes narrow, a mixture of shock and disbelief coursing through me. Lucas must be either very bold or very foolish—maybe both. Annoyed, yet somewhat amused by his audacity, I carefully repack the item and storm over to Lucas's door.

I knock forcefully.

After a moment, Lucas opens the door, wearing an expectant grin that transforms into mock innocence when he sees the re-wrapped parcel in my hands. "Ah, Rosie. Come to say thank you?"

"I don't think that's what I had in mind," I say, thrusting the parcel back at him.

He chuckles as he takes the package from me. "Well, you can't blame a guy for trying to be neighbourly."

"Neighbourly? In my day, a baked cake or casserole was the go-to offer, not a … *this*."

He winks, chuckling as he looks at the brown box in his hands. "Modern problems require modern solutions."

"So, what inspired this particular act of childish pranks? Are you tracking the stress levels in the entire building? Have you paid a visit to Tim?" I ask, gesturing towards Tim's flat. Tim is an older tenant who tends to make offhanded comments towards women. He's the talk of the block most days.

His grin broadens. "Let's just say I felt a disturbance in the force."

I smirk. "Well, let me just warn you: revenge is a dish best served cold."

His eyes sparkle. "s that a promise or a threat?"

"Why not both?" I retort.

He chuckles. "I like your style, Rosie."

"Just wait," I promise, heading back to my flat.

His laughter follows me back to my flat. "Looking forward to it!"

Chapter Six

Tonight, I'm wearing my little black dress with shiny, silver sequins covering the arms and chest. It's not something I usually wear, but I've had it in the back of my wardrobe since my twenty-fifth birthday when Madilyn bought it for me as a gift.

I've taken a black, lacy shawl with me, in case I feel over-dressed, and I'm already using it to cover my arms.

As I walk down the street, I clutch the delicate, black silky shawl in my hands, my steps are hesitant as I decide whether this is a good idea. My mind is racing with thoughts of worthlessness as I wonder if he'll like me, or, will he see the sad-almost-thirty-year-old standing in front of him like a desperate fish in search of water?

Will the conversation be awkward and stilted or will there be a never ending silence, filled with his judgement about my looks or personality. My steps become slower, as if I can somehow delay the inevitable disappointment of my date.

As I turn a corner, about five minutes from the location,

I can't help but steal a glance at my reflection in a nearby shop window. My eyes are wide with a vulnerability I'm too familiar with now, and my cheeks are red from the second hand embarrassment my thoughts are giving me. The shawl, which is now my security blanket, attempts to hide these insecurities, but it's useless. I wear them the same way I wear my dress: for everyone to see.

I'm finally at the address, but I'm sure there's a mistake.

I'm looking up at a giant skyscraper which belongs to a big corporation. Surely, this isn't where I'm supposed to be? Maybe there is a restaurant adjacent to the building, but all I can see are more business offices and a lot of industrial bins. This isn't exactly romantic.

I pull my phone out to message Gabe, asking if he's sent out the wrong address.

I just cannot see the date being here. It's dark, cold, and I'm in a very flashy black dress. Surely life isn't this cruel.

Gabe: Come on up, I'm in Suite 412. My assistant knows you're coming!

A date in his office, he says, because he doesn't want to cancel. It's not a conventional first-date setting, but then again, the conventional dates haven't gone well for me. Maybe this will?

I approach the building, feeling a blend of excitement and nervousness.

I walk up the white corridors, looking at the only splash of colour coming from the artistic, complex art pieces, which I don't really understand. They're dotted all throughout the corridor, leading me towards the elevator, heading towards Suite 412.

I take a deep breath as I step out of the elevator, and it's like I've walked into a completely different office building. This floor is brimming with people. Some are at the photocopier printing out their documents, and others are sitting at their desk answering phone calls and replying to emails. Not one person looks at me as I walk out of the elevator.

I walk towards what looks like the receptionist's desk. She doesn't look up, she just continues typing on her computer, with her expensive gel nails.

"Excuse me?" I ask, politely.

She finishes her sentence, never looking up. Finally, her eyes flash to mine, and she plasters on the fakest smile I think I have ever seen.

"How may I help?" Even her voice is fake.

I pause, distracted by the curtain of a fake facade. "I'm here to see Gabe," I explain.

She looks me up and down, judging my very soul. She's not happy that I'm here.

She looks at her computer and starts to type something. Rolling my eyes, I stand there waiting for some kind of answer.

"Yes, he's ready for you," she spits the words like she's tasted something disgusting.

"Great," I splice, not liking this manner of unprofessional behaviour.

She presses a buzzer, and a man with a smooth, soft voice answers.

"Yes, Crystal?" Oh gosh, she looks and acts like a Crystal.

"A *girl* is here to see you," she announces, the venom still pouring out of her voluminous lips.

Girl? I'm a woman. How insulting.

"Oh, perfect! Send her in!" he answers.

The *girl* at reception sighs but rolls her chair out, and reluctantly stands.

"This way," she says in an unladylike manner. I wouldn't dream of treating someone this way in my job. In fact, I wouldn't treat someone this way—full stop!

"Thank you," I mutter, not wanting to lose my polite demeanour. Some people think my polite manners make me a pushover, or a people pleaser. I think it makes me the opposite. I like to conduct myself in a manner I want others to. I've never shouted at a cold caller, or a waiter or waitress who may have messed up my order. You never know what they've been through in that day, month or year, and it's not my job to make their life worse.

The woman stops at an official looking door, and gestures for me to go in before turning her back and walking off in a huff.

Rolling my eyes, I knock lightly on the door of Suite 412. "Come in," I hear Gabe's voice echo from inside.

Pushing open the door, I find Gabe sitting at his desk, surrounded by stacks of papers and two computer monitors. He looks up and smiles, but it's a smile that doesn't quite reach his eyes.

"Rosie, you made it. Please, have a seat." He gestures to a chair opposite his desk.

The room is filled with the buzz of fluorescent lights and the humming of computers. There's a coldness to the room, an absence of personality, that immediately makes me uneasy. I sit down, subtly pulling my skirt a little lower.

It feels like I'm about to have a job interview as he watches me sit, and I can feel the back of my neck begin to tingle.

"So, Gabe, this is an interesting choice for a date," I say, forcing a smile.

He shrugs. "Well, you know, duty calls. Work doesn't stop just because I've met someone as *fascinating* as you."

I want to believe he's genuine, but there's something in the way he says, *"Fascinating"* that sets off a little alarm bell in my mind. His eyes seem to linger on me a bit too long, as if he's evaluating something more than just my date-worthiness.

"Would you like something to drink? Coffee? Water?" he asks, finally breaking eye contact.

"Water would be great, thanks."

He pours me a glass from a pitcher on a side table. I take a sip, noticing that my hand is shaking slightly. Is it just nerves, or is it the weird vibe I'm getting?

Just as I'm about to ask him about his work, to break the silence, the door bursts open and the receptionist storms in. She's now wearing a headset and looks stressed, her eyes darting between Gabe and me.

"Gabe, we've got a situation that needs—" She stops as her eyes land on me, her expression turning disdainful, "—your attention. It's more important than *this* meeting."

I feel my cheeks turn red, and I suddenly feel like an idiot for thinking this could be a good idea.

Gabe sighs audibly. "Crystal, I told you I was not to be disturbed."

Crystal rolls her eyes. "Well, life doesn't have a pause button, Gabe. Also, this couldn't wait. You have … *someone* on line four. But by all means, continue your "meeting.""

Gabe shoots her a glare and mutters, "Fine. Give me a moment." He turns to me, his annoyed eyes not quite meeting mine. "Rosie, would you mind if we reschedule? It seems like something urgent has come up."

I notice his phone, which is sitting on the table, hasn't buzzed or rung or flashing to show anyone is waiting on line four. It's just there, silent. Coupled with Crystal's sudden intrusion and the odd atmosphere, a feeling of discomfort snakes its way up my spine.

"No, it's fine," I say, placing my glass on the table and picking up my bag. "Actually, I think it's better if we don't reschedule. I'm not sure this is a good fit."

Gabe raises an eyebrow, his charming façade slipping for just a moment to reveal something I can't quite place. "Are you sure?"

Crystal snorts from the doorway, and I suddenly feel like I'm the subject of an inside joke I don't understand.

"Very," I say, meeting Gabe's eyes squarely. "Thank you for the drink."

As I walk past Crystal, she leans into the room and says, "Guess you're not what he's looking for."

I have no idea what she means, and I don't intend on finding out. I quicken my pace, not looking back. My intuition may not always be right, but right now, it's screaming at me to get out of there. And I've learned that sometimes, it's better to listen to that nagging voice in the back of your mind than to ignore it and hope for the best.

As I step into the elevator and press the ground floor button, I let out a sigh of relief. When the doors finally close, separating me from Suite 412 and whatever weirdness was going on there, I feel like I've dodged a bullet.

I don't know exactly what it was—Gabe's intense gaze, the sterile environment, or Crystal's untimely intrusion—but I know I won't be going back to find out.

Sometimes, a bad date is just a bad date, but other times, it's a warning sign. Tonight, it felt like the universe was screaming at me to run. And so I did.

Chapter Seven

Some say love is blind.

But, in my case, it's also hard-of-hearing, with a little extra glitter sprinkled in there for good measure. Love wouldn't be able to see me even if I was screaming for it to notice me whilst I wave my arms around. I could be wearing a massive sign which says, *"Love, I'm right here!"* and it still wouldn't see me.

I wake up to the slow, methodical *tick, tick, tick,* of my internal clock. I can feel it with every beat of my heart. I'm running out of time, and I can feel the sand in my hourglass nearing the bottom. The date last night with Gabe was awful, and reminded me of how dangerous a date can be.

As I lie there, I can still hear the *thump, thump, thump,* and I sit up, sure it's not my imagination.

What the hell?

Nope, it's not the sound of my internal clock, it's the sound of a headboard banging against my bedroom wall. I grab my pillow, attempting to shield my ears from this awful reality.

I check the time and groan. Only Lucas would be banging a woman at six in the bloody morning.

The banging gets faster, and I cannot take another second of the assault on my ears. He ruins my sleep? I will ruin his good time.

I get onto my knees on the bed, and I bang the wall so hard, I feel as though my fist is going to go through the drywall and I'll be face-to-face with Lucas himself. The banging stops. Smiling to myself, I get back into bed, needing another few minutes to cuddle with my pillow and dwell on my life a little more before getting up.

Before I'm even under the sheets, a loud and obnoxious bang comes from his side of the wall. I jump, my heart beating a little faster as I huff, staring at the wall.

The headboard banging against the wall continues louder and faster than before, and something snaps in my tired, and extremely frustrated veins.

Nope, I'm not having this.

I get out of bed, and storm to Lucas's flat. The second I step out of my flat, a cold chill envelops me, sending a shiver down my spine and leaving goosebumps on my skin. Determined, I brave the cold as I slam my front door shut, the sound resonates in the quiet hallway. I pound on Lucas's door, the sound echoing through the corridor. I tap my foot impatiently on the floor as I wait for him to respond.

"Lucas!" I shout when no one comes to the door after a few minutes. I pound on his door again, "I know you're awake!" I shout again, still pounding.

I ignore the curtains opening around me, as the nosey neighbours want to see what all the commotion is about. I can hear dogs barking as my pounding continues.

Eventually, Lucas's door swings open, and I'm face to face with a messy haired, shirtless man, only wearing a loose pair of pyjama bottoms. I have to force myself to keep my eyes on his face.

"Be quiet! Are you trying to wake the entire street?" he whispers angrily, his eyes as wild as his hair. I fold my arms, standing my ground.

"*You* be quiet! All I can hear is you and your new flavour of the week!" I whisper back.

Lucas and I stand there, staring at each other with determination, neither of us backing down. The longer we stand and stare each other down, the more I realise I left my dressing gown hooked on my bedroom door.

Lucas's eyes travel down my oversized t-shirt and bare legs, and I wrap my arms tighter around myself. I lower my eyes for a brief second, my bravado cracking for a mere second.

"You banged on my wall first," he says, his voice still low and deep. I swear he's closer than he was before, but I couldn't be sure.

"Because *you* woke me up with *your* early morning antics, so technically, *you* banged on *my* wall first," I whisper back, poking his chest in accusation. He looks down at my finger and raises his eyebrows at me.

"If you wanted to join in, you should've just asked. Or better yet, do you want that parcel back?" he whispers in amusement. My cheeks burn red at his disgusting notion.

"You are disgusting," I say, scrunching my nose at him.

He steps closer to me. He's so close that I can smell his minty breath and hear his ragged breathing. My eyes feel heavy and my mind hazy.

"I don't think you believe that," he says in his deep, gravelly

62

voice. His eyes dip to my lips, and I find myself forgetting why I came to his flat in the first place. Before I can even attempt a comeback, a woman calls from inside his flat, breaking whatever spell he has created.

"Are you coming back to bed?"

Lucas pauses, his muscles and body tense and he moves backward, further into his flat—further from me.

"Just a second!" he calls back, his voice shaking slightly.

"Just be quiet," I say, my voice no longer angry as I turn and head back into my flat. I shut the door, refusing to look back at Lucas, standing in his doorway, wanting to admire his form. Once my door is shut, I lean against the cool wood, trying to calm my breathing.

I feel like it's pointless to try and go back to sleep. It's close to seven in the morning, so instead of jumping back into bed, like I very much want to, I head into the shower, and wash off this morning.

Once I'm back in my room, I'm glad to hear there's no more banging or other strange, incredibly annoying sounds coming from the other side of the wall.

My phone shrills, announcing an incoming call. Groaning, I grab my phone, noticing that I should probably hoover under my bed soon. I swipe "Answer" without checking the ID.

"Hello?" I ask, my throat groggy from waking up at a stupid hour and shouting at Lucas through his flat door.

"Rosie! Hi!" A woman shrills. I frown, not recognising the voice. I check the caller ID and my heart freezes. It's Julia, Madilyn's mother—my aunt.

"Hi, Auntie Julia! What can I do for you? I'm just about to head into work," I say, completely lying and pretending like I'm not sitting on my messy bed, still in my pyjamas.

"This shouldn't take long! You're always rushing!" she exclaims, and I have to force myself to take deep, steadying breaths. I love Madilyn with every fibre of my being, but her mother? I don't even think they're related.

"We have an appointment this afternoon to try on your bridesmaid dress!" she says it as if I knew about this appointment—I did not. In fact, I don't even remember Madilyn asking me to be her bridesmaid, but I'm honoured all the same.

"Why are we trying them on so early?" I ask.

"Don't worry, it's just to make sure we get the dress in time, and it's not like you will go up two sizes before the wedding!" she says, chuckling to herself. *Breathe, slow and steady*.

"What time?" I ask, knowing how to deal with my family— just smile, show up, and grit my teeth.

"Five. Can you make it?"

"Yeah, sure. Send me the address, and I'll see you there," I say, totally not wanting to go, but I have to show that I'm doing this for Maddy.

"Fabulous! We've got to make sure your dress looks amazing for that new boyfriend of yours. I can't wait to see you guys together at the wedding!" she exclaims, her condescending laugh barrelling down the phone.

I cough, not sure if I heard her right. "I'm sorry, boyfriend?" I ask. I don't remember telling her I found anyone, because I haven't. In fact, I'm too mortified to tell anyone I'm actively looking for a boyfriend in case I fail.

"Yes, Maddy told me the other day that he's coming to the wedding! Very exciting! I best be off, so much to plan!" She hangs up.

I keep my breathing steady. I don't believe that Maddy would tell her mother that I found someone when I didn't.

Would she?

I dial her number, needing answers.

Now.

"Hey bitch," she says.

"Did you tell your mother I have a boyfriend and that he's coming to the wedding?" I ask. Maddy chokes over the phone and doesn't speak for a few seconds as she sorts herself out.

"I'm sorry! She was asking if you had anyone, and it just slipped out. I feel awful!" she says, really sounding like she made a mistake and regretted it.

"Slipped out? Maddy, this isn't like accidentally adding too much salt to a recipe. This is my personal life we're talking about," I say, my voice tinged with both irritation and disbelief. I just cannot believe she'd do this. She knows what my family are like better than anyone... Because they're hers too!

"I know, Rosie. I know. It was a stupid thing to do," Maddy admits, her voice apologetic.

"Stupid doesn't even begin to cover it. Do you know how awkward and humiliating this is going to be? I'm going to show up alone, and then I'll have to explain to everyone, including Aunt Julia, why the imaginary boyfriend you conjured up isn't there!"

"I'll fix it, Rosie. I swear, I'll call her right back and say I made a mistake," Maddy offers hastily.

I quickly jump in. "No, I'll figure something out. It's not just about correcting your 'mistakes.' It's about trust." I feel a knot tightening in my stomach.

Maddy lets out a long sigh. "I honestly didn't think it would be such a big deal. I thought maybe it would even be a bit of fun for you to have people think you're seeing someone."

"Fun? Making me the subject of gossip and speculation is fun to you?" I pause, letting my words sink in. "You have a very strange definition of fun, Maddy."

"I messed up, Rosie. I'm sorry, what else can I say?" She sounds defeated.

I sigh, unable to stay mad at her. "I accept your apology. I guess I'm going to have to find someone sooner rather than later." And I have no leads at all. Every date I've been on has been one disaster after the next.

"Why can't you pay someone to take you?" she suggests, completely serious. A crazier laugh comes out of my mouth as I can't believe what I'm hearing.

"You must be joking! I'm not paying an escort or a prostitute to take me to your wedding. I do still have my pride and self-respect," I insist, shocked she would even suggest such a notion.

"No, I obviously don't mean an escort. I mean asking someone to be your fake boyfriend." She pauses. "I will find someone great for you," she says.

"I appreciate the help and concern, but I really need to do this myself. I have a few more dates to go on, so fingers crossed," I say, not wanting her to feel guilty for making my life a lot harder. I know her mother is a handful and can make you do things without realising you've done it until it's too late. I can't make her feel bad for that.

Plus, it will motivate me to find a match.

"I've got to get to work, speak later?" I ask, feeling deflated. "Sure thing!"

We say our goodbyes and I get up from the safety of my warm, cotton sheets, and I get ready for work.

I settle on my favourite tartan blazer with a maroon turtleneck, deciding it's an appropriate outfit for work and I need to have my head in the game tonight. For some reason, I feel like I'll need it.

Before I leave, I replace the bucket under my bathroom sink, removing the water that is almost spilling over onto my nice new bathroom floor tiles. The sink has been leaking recently and I've been meaning to get it checked out, but I just haven't had the time. A bucket will have to suffice for now.

As I leave my flat, I call Rachel.

"Hey, are you okay?" Rachel asks.

I update her on the Gabe situation, wanting to just get it over with so I can move on with my day. It's a shame Gabe didn't work out, because I generally had high hopes for him.

By the time I'm done, it feels as though my hand is going to fall off under the November chill in London this morning. As soon as the call disconnects, I shove my hands in my pockets, hoping to salvage my fingers by the time I walk into the office. Once I'm there, my hands and face have stopped burning from the stark contrast in temperature.

I head into my office, and I spend most of my day emailing and phoning bloggers and news outlets, getting the word around that *Rachel McStein* is releasing another book. I also write out and plan an entire marketing calendar from now until our estimated launch. Once I'm done, I sit back in my chair and I can feel every muscle in my back is tense, and my fingers stiff from all the typing. My eyes feel dry, and I truly believe I'd feel better if I was hit by a bus.

I look at all the work scattered on my desk, and I find it hilarious how this desk is a literal representation of my life as I remember all the awful dates I've been on. I want this promotion *and* I don't want to be the only woman in the family not to have found love. The stakes feel too high now. The only thing keeping me going on all these degrading dates is the idea that I may just find him. I may find the guy who makes my heart full and my smile wide. As I think about the guy I may meet, I find myself drifting into a daydream.

The man, who remains faceless, is dancing with me at our wedding. No one has judged me or made me feel like an outcast, and life feels sweet—sweeter than our five-tiered, red velvet wedding cake made by Julian Van De Flu, the best cake maker in the entire country.

This dream feels so far away. Almost impossible.

Chapter Eight

"Rosie! I'm so happy to see you!" Julia squeals. I don't miss that voice. The shrill of it goes right through me, sending shivers down my spine.

"Hey, I'm sorry if I'm late."

"Don't be silly! We've only just arrived ourselves! We've been window shopping," she says, the shrill of her voice echoing around the room.

My mother embraces me before she corrects my hair and comments on my poor choice of footwear. Apparently trainers are not appropriate for a dress fitting. I roll my eyes, letting her comments go over my head.

"Rosie, someone told me you found a man?" Grace, Sophia's mother, asks, raising her eyebrows. She bites her lip in anticipation for the confirmation.

Do I lie and say I've found someone? Or do I tell the truth and say I'm still going on dates with no real lead yet?

Usually I tell the truth, but today, as I look at everyone's expectant faces, I panic. No one looks disappointed. Instead, they look excited, which is a look I want to keep. I'm never the one with exciting gossip, and I want it. For some reason, I need this win.

"Yeah, I am," I confirm.

Squeals and claps fill the shop, and everyone surrounds me, barrelling questions at me.

"What's his name?"

"What does he do for a living?"

"Is he cute?"

"When can we meet him?"

All the questions are coming so quickly that they begin to overlap with the other questions and before long, I can't understand anyone and can barely get a word in edgewise.

"I'm glad you finally found someone. I was starting to think I'd failed as a mother!" my mother adds. I can hear the undertones of her message very clearly. God forbid her daughter doesn't have a date to a wedding, because that would make *her* look bad. I love my mother, but she cares too much about what people think, and that's the one thing I've taken from her, and I hate it. I blame my father for cheating on her all this time.

"Okay, okay, everyone stand back and give the girl some space!" Madilyn insists. She's making her way through the group of five women, and she's wearing an incredible, figure-flattering, sophisticated, white sheath dress. The dress is covered in gorgeous lace, with a beautiful, illusion back that takes my breath away. She looks like a real-life princess.

"Madilyn, you look jaw-droppingly gorgeous!" I gasp, taking in the dress and the beautiful woman wearing it. Julia takes a small, white tissue out of her sleeve, and dabs her eyes with it as she takes in her daughter. The other women around me share the astonishment as they take her in, with small gasps of joy.

My problems seem small now, and all I feel is pure happiness for my best friend and cousin.

"Really? You don't think it's too much?" she asks, smoothing the dress over as she looks at herself in a huge mirror which almost touches the ceiling.

"Oh, Madilyn! Don't be silly," Grace insists, her voice is soft and sounds as if she's close to tears.

"Too much doesn't exist on a woman's wedding day! I remember when I got married. I rode to church on the back of a horse and carriage, and my dress was fit enough for a princess," our grandmother says.

"Sophia is terrified of horses, so that's out of the window," Maddy jokes, still looking at herself in the mirror. If I wasn't looking so closely, I wouldn't see the small frown on her forehead.

"You look gorgeous. Besides, if you can't wear too much on your freaking wedding day, then when can you?" I ask, holding my hands together as I watch her smile grow and her eyes twinkle with delight.

"Do you think Sophia will like it?" she asks, chewing her bottom lip in panic. I laugh, walking towards her and taking her hands in mine.

"Stop worrying and enjoy yourself. Sophia will love it and your wedding will be beautiful, okay?" I insist.

"Okay, thank you, guys."

A woman walks out of the back room with a tray of champagne. I take a seat beside Grace and take a glass from the tray. I need this drink after the week I've had.

"So, tell us everything, Rosie," Grace insists, nudging me

slightly.

"About?" I know what she means, but I want to prolong this conversation for as long as possible.

"Who's the man?" she asks again, laughing playfully. All eyes are now on me.

"It's still very new," I say, giving them something, but something tells me that isn't going to be enough for these vultures.

"What's his name?" Julia asks, taking a sip of her champagne and looking at me expectantly.

Crap.

I have no idea what his name is because I haven't met anyone yet. I look over at Maddy, pleading with my eyes for her to help me. She got me in this mess, the least she can do is help me fix it.

"Didn't you say he's taking you out to dinner soon?" Maddy asks. I gave her a look. Is that the best she can do?

"Yeah, I think he's taking me sometime this week."

Grace and Julia share a few glances between each other—they aren't buying it.

"She's shy, that's all! I remember the first time I met my Peter," she pauses, remembering her late husband, and I feel my heart ache for her. "We were so nervous to announce we were courting because he didn't come from a very stable household. We only announced it when we both felt ready. Announcing something before the two of you are even sure this is going to last, is very daunting. Let's give Rosie some space with it and hopefully we meet him at the wedding," our grandmother says, giving me a kind and understanding smile.

Part of me feels relieved and thankful for my grandmother, but an even bigger part feels guilty.

Chapter Eight

I shift in my seat, "Thank you. I just want to see where this goes," I confirm, taking a big gulp of my champagne.

"Well, I can't wait to meet him and to hear all about it when you're ready!" she says, and that pang of guilt stabs me again. Julia and Grace look disappointed, but I'm glad the topic seems to have switched.

"Who is the bridesmaid?" the woman who brought us champagne asks. I look at her name tag for a name.

"That would be me, Paula," I say. She gives me a small smile and nod, before she gestures for me to follow her into the changing rooms.

"I hope you love the dress," Maddy says, chewing her bottom lip again.

"I'm sure it'll be perfect," I reassure her, hoping I'm right. I really don't want to look like a marshmallow. I just have to remind myself that this is Maddy's day, not mine.

I enter the changing room and as Paula pulls the curtain across behind me, I'm face to face with a white garment cover, hiding the dress from sight.

"Are you ready to see the dress Madilyn has chosen for you?" she asks, her hand hovering over the zipper.

I gulp. "Go for it."

She slowly uncovers the dress, and I release a breath as the dress turns out to be a stunning A-Line, emerald silk dress which reaches the floor and showing off my figure. It's stunning, and exactly my style.

"Well?" Maddy calls out, worry laced in her voice.

"You'll have to see when I come out!" I shout back as I strip down to my underwear. Paula places the dress over my head, helping me to navigate the sleeves and shoulders so I don't rip the delicate fabric.

"Do you like it?" she calls out again.

"I'll show you when I'm out!" I repeat. I hear her huffing and puffing from the other side of the curtain, and I can't help but laugh. This is what she gets for making me lie to my family.

Once the dress is on, Paula uncovers the mirror and I find myself speechless. Even though my hair isn't styled, and my make-up isn't done, I look beautiful. It's not often I say that about myself, but this dress feels like it's made just for me to wear it.

I stand in front of the full-length mirror,. the emerald dress clinging to me like a second skin, showing off the figure I very rarely show off.

With one last look in the mirror, I nod to Paula to peel back the curtain.

Gasps and claps and other forms of endearment and showered my way. I can't help the blush from forming on my cheeks as I take in everyone's comments.

"You look gorgeous!"

"Like a true angel."

"Your new boyfriend will be very happy when he sees you dressed like that!"

At the sound of the word "boyfriend," my heart does a mini somersault in my chest, and the moment has erupted in flames.

"You truly look amazing. I knew that colour would compliment your skin tone!" Maddy enthuses, feeling the silk, emerald material.

"Stand together you two, we need to take a photo of the bride and bridesmaid!" Julia says, waving her phone in the air.

We move closer and wrap our arms around each other. As the flash goes off, my mother claps her hands, looking at me with a mixture of pride. "You do look beautiful. I just hope this new boyfriend is going to treat you well."

I nod, my smile fading slightly. I know exactly where this is going. My mother has always been a mixture of encouraging and cautious, as if she wasn't sure what was best for me. She wants me with a man, but also warns me of the dangers, since my father cheated on her.

I sigh, knowing she only means well and is only looking out for me. "I'll be careful. He's different," I say, the guilt of lying cutting through me like a knife.

My mother smiles. "I just want you to be happy, to find someone who loves you as much as you deserve, and nothing less."

Aunt Julia chimes in, giving me a playful nudge. "We've got your back, too. If he hurts you, he has the whole family to answer to!"

Maddy cuts in, seeing my obvious discomfort. "I was meaning to ask, Rosie. On the day of my wedding, can you come to the bridal suite at the venue in the morning before the ceremony starts? I'd love your help and encouragement," she asks. I'm grateful she's moved the topic from me to her, as it should be.

"Yes, of course! I'll be there."

Chapter Nine

It's been a few days since Lucas and the "parcel incident," and I've been racking my brain for the perfect revenge plan. It hits me as I'm sitting on my sofa, watching a repeat of my comfort show: pizza. Everybody loves pizza, but nobody loves an unexpected avalanche of it at their doorstep.

I pick up my phone, pull up the local pizza delivery website, and order twenty pizzas to Lucas's address, opting to pay with cash once they arrive.

I give them Lucas's address, and they confirm that the delivery will arrive within the hour. I can barely contain my excitement as I open up the window, and peer out from behind the curtain, waiting for the pizza delivery car to show up. I can't see Lucas's door, but I'll be able to hear it.

Finally, it arrives. I can hear the elevator doors open and I see as the pizza delivery guy heads towards Lucas's flat. My view is obstructed a bit, but I can see half of Lucas's door, which is enough.

Knock, knock, knock.

My skin erupts in goosebumps as I hear Lucas open the door. I can imagine his initial expression of curiosity melting into one of sheer confusion as he sees the mountain of pizza boxes.

"Are you Lucas?" the driver asks, seemingly unfazed by Lucas's flabbergasted face.

"I am," Lucas nods.

"I've got your order of twenty pizzas. Where would you like them?"

At this moment, I feel like a criminal. A criminal who is going to be caught and their crimes revealed to the entire world. I can imagine the police storming towards my flat and arresting me on the spot. I can see a lifetime behind bars, and as I'm thinking of this potential future, I ask myself the question: was it worth it?

Yes. It was.

"I'm sorry, mate. There seems to be a misunderstanding. I haven't ordered

any pizzas," Lucas says—his voice muffled through the glass.

The pizza delivery guy disappears from my view, returning without the boxes. He must have placed them down somewhere. He checks his phone for the order, I'm assuming, and shows Lucas the screen.

"It's definitely for this flat, see?" he asks, pointing to whatever it says on the phone.

Lucas comes into view, stepping out of his flat, and he's looking right at me. I squeal and hide behind the wall beside the window, knowing he saw me. My blinds are still swinging from my abrasive retreat.

I bang my head on the wall, knowing he's going to figure out it's me. If it wasn't obvious before, it's obvious now.

I can hear their muffled chatter, but because I'm further away from the window, I can barely make out the words. Biting my lip, I make the decision to peek through the blinds, just to see what is happening, and if Lucas is still staring at my flat.

When I'm finally able to see outside, through the tiny gaps left by my blinds, the pizza delivery guy is walking down the stairs, without any pizza boxes in sight.

I squeal and jump back from the window again as Lucas' face comes into view. His face is thunderous as he looks at me through the slats of my dancing blinds. His jaw is clenched, and his eyebrows are formed in a straight line.

He taps on the window with his nail, summoning me out of my flat.

That's it—the jig is up.

He knows I'm here, thanks to my traitor blinds, so I may as well go outside and face the music.

I open the door, throwing on the best poker face I can muster. "Looks like you're having a pizza party, Lucas. Mind if I join?"

His eyes dart to mine as he places his hand on my door frame. I can hear the wood cracking under his palm as he leans forward, his intense eyes boring into mine.

"Do you want to know what's funny?" he asks, his voice is sarcastic, but I can hear a humorous undertone. I catch a whiff of his cologne, distracting me for a moment—it's almost too much. But, the way he's looking at me is enough to snap me back.

I grin, scratching my forearm. "What's funny?" I ask, delaying the inevitable.

"When you order online but change the address, it doesn't change the account name of the account holder," he explains, leaning closer again.

"I don't know what you're talking about," I say, sticking to my guns.

Lucas's laugh comes out like a grumble from the depths of his chest. "Really?" he asks.

I can't help but laugh at his bewildered expression. "Call it a neighbourly" gesture. Modern problems require modern solutions, right?"

For a moment, he's speechless, studying the mountain of pizza boxes as if contemplating the logistics of what he's going to do with them. Then he bursts into laughter.

Lucas shakes his head, grinning widely now. "I thought being 'neighbourly' was borrowing cups of sugar?"

I laugh. "Ah, sugar, flour, a dozen pizzas—what's the difference?" I say, my eyes twinkling with mischief. "I'm just trying to make sure you don't go hungry."

He chuckles, pushing a pizza box toward me. "I will never eat all of this alone so shall we share pizza? Any preference?" he asks.

I eye up the pizza boxes, and choose a random one at the top. "What are you going to do with the rest?" I ask, conscious of the potential waste.

"We can go around, offering the neighbours some?" he suggests.

"We?" I ask, raising my eyebrows.

"Yep. You wanted to be 'neighbourly' after all."

I can't help but laugh at his response. "Fair enough, let's be the pizza fairy godparents of this flat building."

I place my pizza box in my flat before we each take a few boxes and step into the hallway of our building. It feels strange, delivering pizzas with Lucas, but it's the most fun I've had in a while.

Lucas knocks on the first door and Martha answers. She's a

woman in her late thirties who has two children under the age of ten. She always says 'hello' when we pass by in the elevator. She gives us a tired but genuine smile. "Hi, we have some extra pizzas. Would you like one?" Lucas asks, holding out a box.

Her eyes widen with surprise. "Oh, my goodness! Really? That would be fantastic—the kids will be thrilled!"

"You're welcome. Enjoy!" I say, handing her the box.

We wave goodbye and continue down the hallway, knocking on another door. This time, Richard, an older man, answers. "Pizza, you say?" he asks, eyes narrowing.

"Yep! Freshly delivered and untouched. We ordered way too much, and didn't want them going to waste," Lucas assures him.

"Well, that's mighty neighbourly of you Lucas," Richard says, taking the box and giving us a nod. Richard has recently lost his wife, so I'm happy we can do something nice for him.

As we make our way through the building, handing out pizzas, I think it would be a perfect time to get to know Lucas a bit more.

"So, Lucas, what do you do for work?" I ask, curious to know what a guy like Lucas does day-to-day.

"I'm a journalist. What about you?" he asks, genuinely interested.

"I'm a marketing manager. So, pretty much buried in social media and spreadsheets most of the time," I explain.

"Ah, a fellow creative," he teases.

We reach the last door, and Lucas knocks. Amanda and David answers, looking between Lucas and I, puzzled but intrigued.

"Hi Amanda! We're going around giving out pizzas. Would you like one?" I ask, giving her a warm smile. Amanda and

David have recently moved in, and they seem like a lovely couple. I see them holding hands and embracing each other from my window, and it reminds me how lonely I am.

Sad.

They exchange a glance and then both burst out laughing. "Hi Rosie, we were just debating what to have for dinner. You're a lifesaver!" says the guy, taking the last pizza box from Lucas.

Out of pizza and the aroma of melted cheese and warm dough clinging to our clothes, we start to walk back to our flat. Our footsteps slow as we reach our doors.

I shift my pizza box from one hand to the other, and grab the door handle. "Thank you for a fun evening, I guess?" I say, unsure of what this evening actually was.

Lucas chuckles. "You mean, thank you for stopping the food waste which would have resulted from your prank?" he asks, teasing. "In that case, you're welcome."

I laugh. "Shut up. You literally ordered me a…" I pause, cringing at the thought of saying it out loud.

"A what?" He asks, smirking as he clearly takes pleasure in my discomfort.

"You know what! Now I consider we're even."

He raises his eyebrow. "Maybe, maybe not."

"I think you should sleep with one eye open," I tease, my heart fluttering a little faster as his laugh engulfs the hall.

He grins, his eyes twinkling mischievously. "I'll be ready for whatever you throw my way."

I turned to unlock my flat door, feeling an emotion I haven't felt before. I'm not sure what it is, but I'll be interested to find out. Before stepping inside, I look back at Lucas, who is still standing in the hallway. "Goodnight, Lucas," I say, my voice softening.

He nods, his expression becoming more serious. "Good-night, Rosie." There is a moment of hesitation before he adds, "And thank you for tonight. It was … different."

I can't help but wonder if he means it was different because of the prank or if there was something more he wanted to say. But I don't press further, I simply smile and step into my flat.

As I settle on my sofa, surrounded by the remnants of my pizza prank, I can't deny that I was looking forward to getting to know Lucas a little more.

Chapter Ten

"You know, maybe this is it?" Elijah says, looking at the next guy I recently matched with. I agreed to go for dinner this evening, but now I wish I didn't. I'd rather sit at home, watching some trashy T.V. and finding other ways to annoy Lucas than sit through another wasted evening of disappointment and embarrassment.

I rub my arms again, wishing I brought my jacket. I can picture it hanging up near my front door on a hook, and I can almost imagine the warmth it provides me with. Dresses are not warm, especially during wintertime in London.

"I don't know. To be honest, I'm losing hope in this whole thing," I say, rubbing my arms as a draft whips through the café.

"Shut up and go. You have nothing to lose," he says, putting a glass under the bar.

"I might have nothing to gain, too," I say, unable to stop being sceptical. I've never had any luck with men, so why would I now?

"Rosie, I'm going to disown you in a minute. Have some faith, okay?" When I don't reply, still sitting on the stool feeling sorry for myself, Elijah sighs. "Do you think I've had it easy? I remember when I was in college, and I came out as gay, no one would even look at me. I mean, you remember! Even the guys who were gay, but hadn't come out yet, would make fun of me. But did that last forever?" he asks. "No! You just have to be patient and understand that your time will come."

I grab his hand, remembering how hard college was for him. He never once complained, and now look at me, complaining about a few bad dates.

"I'm sorry, I'll try, I promise," I say, squeezing his hand. That's the pep talk I needed, now I feel ready and prepared to slay this date. I think.

"Call me if it flops and we'll all go out for a few drinks, yeah?" he suggests.

"Okay, sounds good." I need a night out this week. I grab my bag and stand up from my stool, already dreading the cold I'm about to be subjected to.

"I better get going. Wish me luck," I say.

"I would say 'break a leg' but knowing your luck?" he shouts back, causing me to chuckle.

"Yeah right, I've never broken a bone in my entire body!"

"Tonight could be the night!" His voice fades as the door closes behind me.

As soon as I'm out of the warm cafe, I shiver and my teeth chatter. The wind is starting to pick-up and I rub my arms as I walk towards the restaurant. I thank God that it isn't too far away, but I still regret leaving my coat.

Once my eyes land on the warm, well-lit restaurant, I begin to run as my fingers start to become numb from the cold.

I burst through the doors, people turning to look at me with a dirty, confused look as I interrupt the peace. I mutter a whispered apology, not caring that I'm making a scene right now. It's freezing.

"Can I help you?" a waiter asks and makes a gesture to ask for my coat but stops himself as he notices my lack of coat.

I give him a small smile, looking around the restaurant for a man wearing a denim jacket and a London bridge badge on the chest pocket. That's what Craig said he will be wearing.

"I'm waiting for a guy named Craig?" I ask, hoping Craig is already here and has made them aware that a woman would be coming in, looking for him.

But by the look of confusion on the waiter's face, I'm going to assume that has not happened.

"It's okay, is there a waiting room?" I ask, just glad for the warmth of the restaurant. He nods and ushers me over to some sofas.

"Thank you," I say, taking a seat. I pull my phone out and check the time. He's only ten minutes late, so maybe he's stuck in some traffic?

As ten minutes turn into thirty minutes, I begin to think about all the things that can go wrong on *this* date:

1. He goes on about all his exes, and I'm wishing I could teleport out of this restaurant.
2. He's not the guy in his profile picture. Instead, he's at least fifty years old, balding, and divorced five times and I've experienced my first ever catfish.
3. A never-ending amount of awkward silence which is my worst fear.
4. He goes for a kiss on the cheek, but I mistake his

intentions and kiss his lips and he never calls me back again.

But out of all these options, I never expected to be stood up.

I stare at my phone for the umpteenth time. I've been sitting in this rather upscale restaurant for almost forty-five minutes, nursing a glass of sparkling water and nibbling on a breadstick. Around the twenty-five minute mark, I sent a text to Craig, *"I'm here, table near the window,"* but my phone continues to lie on the white linen tablecloth, with no message back. I considered sending another message, but the little voice inside my head said, *"Don't be desperate."* I scroll through our conversation, and, even though we didn't talk for days or hours, he seemed interesting and nice. He didn't seem like the kind of guy who would stand someone up.

Finally, I flag down the waiter, forcing a smile.

"Any sign of him?" I ask.

He shakes his head, and offers me a glass of wine—on the house. *Christ, how embarrassing, they feel bad for me.*

"No, thank you. I won't waste any more of your time. Thank you," I say, too embarrassed to stay any longer. I ask for the bill for my sparkling water and breadsticks. I feel a flood of humiliation wash over me as I put on my coat. I know I'm the subject of whispered conversations among the restaurant staff and a few of the more observant diners. Holding back tears, I hurriedly pay and leave, letting the door close behind me.

The cobblestone streets underfoot reverberated with the staccato of my heels, each click echoing the conflicting thoughts bouncing around in my mind. How could he stand me up? What's next—drowning sorrows in ice cream and a trite romcom? Or perhaps something a bit more sophisticated—a glass of wine and a soak in a hot bath?

Still deep in thought, I round the corner, enveloped by the golden glow of the antique street lamps. I bump—quite ungracefully—into Lucas.

"Whoa there!" he exclaims, steadying me by my arms just as my heel catches between two cobblestones, sending me into a wobbly dance. In an unfortunate twist of fate—or maybe just my luck—I lose my balance completely and stumble.

Time seems to slow as I fall, bracing for the impact I know is waiting for me. Let's be honest, it's the perfect end to a really crappy night. But the impact never comes. Instead, Lucas catches me, pulling me into his chest with an arm wrapped securely around my waist. I gasp as I hit his strong, hard body, grabbing onto his forearms for support.

"I'm so sorry," he apologises, his eyes filled with concern as he helps me stand upright. "Are you alright?"

"I'm fine," I mumble, my cheeks flushing with embarrassment and my heart pounding for a completely different reason now. "Just a bit frazzled tonight, I guess."

He stands there, dressed in casual elegance with a collared shirt and jeans, a smile playing at the corners of his mouth. He holds a bag of take out, but he still manages to steady me.

His eyes flicker down, surveying my dress—a black, slinky number I had chosen specifically for the romance that never materialised tonight. "You look gorgeous. Hot date?" he inquires, a touch of discomfort lacing his tone as he continues to observe me in the dress. His eyes, going over my every curve.

I blush as I watch him watch me, the air leaving my lungs as I remember what happened tonight. "Something like that. More like a no-show date."

Lucas raises an eyebrow as his softening eyes meet mine in the ambient light. "Their loss, obviously," he says, gesturing to my dress again. "Hey, you hungry?"

The words hung in the air like a trapeze, waiting to be caught. I like Lucas, there was no doubt about it, but tonight was supposed to be about candlelight, soft jazz, and sparks flying across a table adorned with crystal and silverware. Lucas is offering friendly banter and the simplicity of take out because he feels sorry for me. Yet, the thought of returning to an empty flat made my decision easier.

"Come on," he coaxes, almost as if reading my hesitation. "I was going to eat this curry alone at my place, and it's always better with company. And look"—he gestures to the bag—"I even have garlic bread and a few sides."

My eyes met his, and in that moment, I saw something else in Lucas. Right now, he isn't my annoying room mate, he's a companion after a really crappy night. Lucas doesn't have an expectation for me, and right now, this is incredibly tempting. The prospect of not being alone tonight began to outweigh the disappointment that had previously filled the evening with my no-show.

"Alright, fine, but only if it's at my place. You can't buy the food and host, especially after buying all that pizza," I agree, striving to keep my face neutral, yet feeling a sense of relief wash over me like the tide reclaiming the shore.

"The pizza wasn't a choice. This is," he says, his eyes sparkling with something I can't quite put my finger on.

When we reach my flat, Lucas places the take out on the dining table—a makeshift setup that has seen more solo dinners than social gatherings—and starts unpacking the food. The scent of the rich Jalfrezi sauce intertwined with the aromatic promise of garlic bread and the spicy potatoes, fills the space with a warmth that is almost palpable.

"I hope you like spicy food," he says, revealing a container filled with jalfrezi sauce. He looks up, locking eyes with me, and for the briefest of moments, the room feels charged, as if a current runs between us.

"I love it," I reply, my heart beating when I realise he bought my favourite meal, without even realising it.

"I thought it might help take the edge off tonight," he continues, trying to look nonchalant but failing. His eyes scan my face, as if searching for signs of how the evening has impacted me. "Food always seems to make things better."

"It's like a hug from the inside," I say, forcing a smile. I watch as Lucas divides the steaming Jalfrezi into two bowls. The sound of the spoon scraping against the container mingles with the awkward silence.

"A hug from the inside," he echoes, as if considering the weight of those words. He grabs the garlic bread and starts laying slices on each plate before grabbing the potatoes and sharing them out. "Do you usually eat alone?"

I hesitate, picking at the frayed edge of the tablecloth. "More often than I'd like to admit."

He stops what he's doing and looks up at me. "Me too," he says, and it's not in a pitiful way, but in a manner that suggests he truly understands the solitary echo that bounces off these walls.

Finally, we sit down, and the food creates a barrier of sorts, something to focus on other than the thick tension in the air. He takes the first bite, savouring the burst of spices as they hit his palate. "How is it?" I ask, hoping the meal will serve as a neutral topic to diffuse the awkwardness.

"Amazing. I've always loved curry. I think it's a great pick me up meal," he says, taking a bite and savouring the taste. "You know," he begins with a mischievous grin, "I once tried to impress a date by ordering the spiciest curry on the menu."

I take a sip of water, almost spitting it back out again. "Are you serious? How did that go?" I ask, laughing as I wipe the water off my chin.

"Let's say it didn't end well for me." He chuckles, his eyes sparkling with amusement.

I lean forward, wanting to know more. "Do tell," I challenge, my eyes daring him to explain further.

He watches me for a moment with a smirk on his face as if he were deciding on what to do. He eventually caves, lowering his voice for dramatic effect. "She didn't believe that I had a high spice tolerance, so I saw it as a challenge to impress her. I ordered the curry feeling pretty confident, only when I took a big bite, my mouth started burning! My face was redder than a tomato! I must have downed three glasses of water in less than a minute. Needless to say, I didn't get a second date."

I burst into laughter, and he joins in, wiping our eyes with our napkins as tears start to form in our eyes.

"What about you?" he asks, clearing his throat as his laughter subsides.

I take another sip of water. "What do you mean?"

"Any notable dates?" he asks, leaning back in his chair, seemingly intrigued by this conversation.

I chug more water, suddenly feeling awkward as I remember my awful encounters. My cheeks go red as I think about them. "Let's just say I've had *terrible* dates," I say, hoping he doesn't pry more.

"Do tell," he says, his eyes glinting with that mysterious

sparkle I'm beginning to recognise.

I sigh, deciding it *is* fair I share at least one of mine. Besides, they do make a good story. "I don't think it's as good as yours, but I went on a date in this guy's office…" I say, thinking he'll take that.

He doesn't.

He leans forward, wanting more information.

I chuckle. Surely this isn't that interesting. "His receptionist clearly had a crush on him and kept interrupting us, so I left. And that's it! Not as good as your story, but I don't have many to tell,"

"That is very interesting! Meeting a guy in his office is clearly a red flag, right?" He asks this as if I already know the answer. I do *now*, but I didn't know *then*.

Our conversation shifts to childhood memories, and I find myself giggling as Lucas recounts an embarrassing story from his childhood.

"So, picture this," he begins, his eyes twinkling with laughter. "I was about nine years old, and I had a massive crush on my neighbour, so I decided to write her a love letter."

I lean in, eager to hear the juicy details. "Go on."

Lucas's cheeks turn a faint shade of pink. "I poured my heart out in that letter, professing my undying love. The next day, I gave it to her, and she burst out laughing. She showed all the kids in school, and I found out I had misspelt half the words, and my handwriting was a mess. I was mortified."

"Did you recover from the embarrassment?" I ask, feeling bad for young Lucas.

He grins. "I did. I actually became very popular in college, and she asked me out. But let's just say she never let me forget that letter."

Our conversation flowed effortlessly from one topic to another, from embarrassing moments to dreams and aspirations. I don't think I've ever spoken to Lucas this much before, and I like it. He's interesting, and he's not shy to open up about his life. I can't stop the feelings of butterflies flying around in my stomach every time he looks at me.

"Okay, Rosie," Lucas says, his expression turning serious for a moment. "What's one thing you've always dreamed of doing but haven't had the chance to yet?"

I pause, considering his question. "I've always wanted to become the Chief of Marketing in my company, which might happen if I can up my numbers." I say.

Lucas shakes his head. "No, something that has nothing to do with work. Something that's unique and something not everyone can do."

I pause again, realising I do have something weird I've always wanted to do. "Well, there's this one thing I've always wanted to do, but it's a bit … weird."

He leans in, curiosity dancing in his eyes. "I'm all ears."

I take a deep breath, my voice filled with excitement as I blurt it out. "I've always wanted to go on a hot air balloon ride. You know, floating high above the world, with nothing but the vast sky around you. It just seems so magical, and nothing can bother you from up there."

Lucas's eyes light up with genuine interest. "That sounds incredible. I've never been on a hot air balloon either. Maybe one day we can cross that off both our bucket lists."

The idea of going on a hot air balloon with Lucas makes me feel excited. "I'd love that," I reply with a smile.

As we continued to talk and share stories, the evening seemed to stretch on, but I wasn't in a rush.

Chapter Ten

Chapter Eleven

"I cannot believe he stood you up," Madilyn gasps, her eyes and mouth wide with shock. We met up at Pandemonium, a club we've been going to since we finished university. This place has seen a lot of dramas, but it's also seen a lot of the good old days.

"What. A. Massive. Ass." Elijah claps, emphasising each word.

"Is no one going to comment on the poetry guy? I mean, unhinged!" Sophia comments, her face scrunching in disdain as she recounts the story I've been telling them all night.

"I told you I have no luck with dating!" I groan, sinking further into the red leather sofa, which was slightly sticky from the copious amounts of spilled drinks and god knows what else it had been subjected to over the years. As I sink into the sofa, I can't help but smile at the thought of what happened afterwards. The thought of Lucas coming to my place and sharing his take out with me warmed my heart, and I can't stop smiling each time I think of it. But I don't think I'll tell my friends, in case they read into it a bit too much.

"You just have to keep trying." I give Maddy a look to say she has no idea what I'm going through. "Don't you think I've never had awful dates! Don't you remember Elizabeth?" she asks, looking over her shoulder to check to see that her fiancée, Sophia, is still at the bar, grabbing us some drinks.

"Oof, you avoided a very expensive heartbreak, and psychotic episode," Elijah says, as we remember Lizzie. Maddy and Lizzie didn't even go on a first date, she met her online and they decided to meet up and go ice-skating only for her brother to show up saying she can't make it.

"Oh yeah, that was pretty messy," I say, cringing a little as I remember that whole ordeal.

"At least you're getting married now. I can't say that for me," I argue.

She rolls her eyes. "My point is, you have to kiss a lot of frogs before you find someone you can tolerate for most of your life," Maddy says.

"Tolerate?" Sophia questions as she comes up behind Maddy, holding a tray of our drinks.

"You know I love you," Maddy promises, before Sophia leans in and kisses her forehead.

"You two make me sick!" I joke, taking my drink and not hesitating in taking a very large sip.

"What are we talking about?" Sophia asks, sitting on the chair next to Maddy.

"My sad, sad love life," I say, ignoring Elijah's and Maddy's snickers.

"He stood her up," Maddy whispers to Sophia. Sophia's eyebrows lift and her face screams, *"Yikes,"* as she takes in my disappointing form.

"Honey, you'll find someone, trust me. Even if it takes you a few more years, you'll find the one who makes you laugh so much your stomach hurts," she says, holding onto Maddy's hands.

"I don't have years. I have months!"

"Months?" she asks, looking between everyone.

Doesn't she know what Maddy told her mother?

My eyes flick to Maddy, and her face gives me the answer.

"Tell Sophia what you've subjected me to," I say, crossing my arms over my chest.

"I said I'm sorry!" she defends, not looking Sophia in the eye.

"What did you tell Julia?" Sophia asks, mimicking me and crossing her arms across her chest.

"Well," she says, stuttering as she tries to find the words.

"She told Julia that I've found a man and I'm bringing him to your wedding!" I reveal, still slightly annoyed about it. I forgave her, but after being stood up, I'm even further away from meeting anyone I can take to their wedding. Plus, if I don't find anyone, everyone is going to think I got dumped by the guy. That's just what I need.

Sophia looks her in the eye. "You didn't, Mads." Sophia gasps, her eyes becoming wide as she realises that she did in fact do this.

"I said I was sorry, but it just came out. You know what my mother is like!" she says, taking a large sip of her drink.

"Yeah, but Julia becomes quite obsessive over this kind of thing. Don't you remember what she was like when we first got together?" she asks, tutting. Maddy sinks further into her sticky chair.

"What did she do when you guys first started dating?" Elijah asks—he has been sitting down watching us women bicker over men with a big smirk on his face.

"She used to time our visits."

"Time your visits?" he repeats, sitting up straighter in his chair, fully engrossed in the conversation.

"Yep. I was only allowed a few hours with Mads in the evening when she was still living with Julia, and she would time my visits."

Elijah bursts out laughing.

"Plus, when Sophia asked Julia if she could propose to me, my mother insisted Sophia take her to choose the ring."

"Insisted? She basically forced me! If I didn't take her, I couldn't propose!"

"You see? I love Aunt Julia, but she is not the kind of woman you want to lie to!" I exclaim, thinking about the possibility of Julia finding out there is no man in my life.

"Just take me as your date," Elijah suggests once he's finished laughing.

"Have you forgotten the fact that she knows who you are, and that you're openly gay?" I ask, scratching the back of my hand. When I'm feeling really overwhelmed, the back of my hand gets incredibly itchy.

"Oh yeah," he says, sitting back in his chair.

"What am I going to do? I need a date for your wedding, but I'm seriously running out of time."

"Rosie?"

My back stiffens and my heart starts beating a little faster as that deep voice runs through my body like an electric current, causing me to shiver. I stop scratching my hand and look to my left, where Lucas is standing, right beside Elijah.

"Lucas? What are you doing here?" I ask, totally caught off

guard. My voice trembles slightly as I remember the magical night we just shared.

"I'm just out with some guys from work." He doesn't ask me what I'm doing here, he just leans over, greeting Elijah.

"Hi, mate," he says to Elijah, shaking his hand. As he does, I catch a whiff of his musky, sweet aftershave and I swear my eyes almost rolled to the back of my head. My head became dizzy and fuzzy, but I know it's because of the alcohol...

"I would offer to make you your regular hot chocolate, but I'm off duty," Elijah says, holding his hands up in fake defence, a grin spreading along his face.

"Don't worry, I won't hold it against you," Lucas jokes.

"Aren't you going to introduce us?" Maddy asks, already holding her hand out to Lucas.

"This is Lucas," I say, gesturing towards the tall, looming man behind me.

"This is Madilyn, my cousin, and her fiancée, Sophia."

They both shake his hand, smiling like they know something I don't.

"Call me, Maddy," Maddy says, settling back in her seat. The way she said it made it sound like she was insinuating something dirty.

"Nice to meet you both," he says, a small chuckle leaving his soft, plump lips.

"How do you two know each other?" Sophia asks, her eyes flickering between us both.

Before I can answer, Lucas buts in. "We're neighbours," he says.

"How long have you lived next door to Rosie, Lucas?" Sophia asks, smiling wide at Lucas.

"A year, maybe?" he says, turning his head to look at me and waiting for me to confirm.

I nod, my brain cannot stop thinking about last night.

"How come I've never bumped into you, then?" she asks.

He clears his throat. "I tend to work late," he says, taking another swig of his beer.

Before I can formulate another question, Lucas glances over his shoulder. Following his gaze, I see his friends at the bar, laughing and downing shots like there's no tomorrow.

"I should get back to my friends before they drink this bar out of alcohol," he says. Then his eyes find mine. The thought of that embarrassing night years ago vanishes—the room around us seems to dim. It's just me and him, the same Lucas who generously shared his meal with me yesterday after my date stood me up.

His eyes glisten, shining with a mixture of curiosity and earnestness, as he offers me a smile that causes me to shiver. I'm aware that my friends are here, that this could be socially awkward, but none of that matters. I smile back, regardless of my confused feelings. The room might as well be empty. In that moment, as fleeting as it may be, the chemistry is undeniable. Then he breaks the spell with a small nod, turning back to join the raucous laughter of his friends, but the moment lingers, humming in the air like a sweet melody long after he's gone.

"Wow … What was that? He's so cute," Maddy whispers to me, still looking after the gap Lucas disappeared in.

Sophia gently smacks her arm, laughing at her fiancée. "Stop it, you," she says, shaking her head.

I rub my arms, resisting the urge to find Lucas in the crowd.

"He's a nightmare," is all I say before we turn the conversation into less complicated things.

Five shots down, seven vodka and cokes, and a cheeky glass of red wine, I can barely see straight.

Bathed in the dim, kaleidoscopic light, I twirl gracefully through a sea of swaying bodies. I dance with Elijah, Maddy, and Sophia, yet, my attention is tethered to another corner of the room. There, Lucas leans against the bar, his tall silhouette framed by a halo of blues and smoky purples, a living, breathing Van Gogh painting of swirling lights. I pretend to be distracted, attempting to hide my interest behind fluttering lashes and a laugh I share with my friends, but the charade is paper-thin. We both know that I am irrevocably drawn to him.

Time slows down with every twirl and every step I take on the dance floor. It's as though I've tumbled back in time to when I was twenty-one.

From across the room, Lucas leans against the bar, the dim light casting shadows on his features. His eyes, however, remain luminous, almost fixated as they catch sight of me. He brings his beer to his lips, taking a slow sip as if savouring the moment as much as the drink. There's an undertone of hunger in that gaze, a yearning that's hard to define but impossible to ignore.

He laughs with his friends occasionally, but his eyes keep returning to me, like a compass needle finding its true north. In my drunken haze, those glances aren't casual; they're full of intent, as if he's absorbing every movement I make, every flicker of my dress, every toss of my hair.

I feel his eyes on me when I spin around in jubilant circles, the floor, sticky beneath my heels. It's as though his gaze itself propels me, urging me to dance like I've never danced before. And I do.

Lucas smiles, a subtle curve of his lips that I've come to recognise. It's a smile that says he knows exactly what this dance is, what these stolen glances mean. Whenever his gaze drifts away, I find myself chasing the feel of his eyes on me— wanting him to lock eyes with me once more, craving the soft curvature of his lips. A voice in my head, gentle but insistent, whispers that it's merely the alcohol, the atmosphere, the intoxicating blend of sight and sound. But somewhere deeper, nestled in a sacred chamber of my heart, I know it might be something more.

"Do you want another drink?" Sophia shouts over the booming music. I regretfully tear my eyes off of Lucas to answer.

"I'll grab them," I shout back, using this as an excuse to speak to Lucas at the bar. I feel on top of the world. I haven't thought about being stood up, and the stakes of finding a date has, instead, I've let myself enjoy the night, dancing with friends and allowing myself to let go.

"Are you sure?" she shouts again, laughing as Maddy takes Sophia in her arms and twirls her around Elijah.

I laugh. "Yeah, you stay here! What do you all want?" I ask, finishing the last drop of my vodka and coke. I pull a face as the vodka is stronger than I thought it was.

"Two vodka and cokes, and Malibu and lemonade, please!" Elijah asks, waving his arms to the beat of the music.

I laugh. "You got it."

I navigate through the pulsing crowd of sweaty bodies, the bass of the music thumping in my chest. The air is thick with the aroma of sweat and alcohol, but my focus is on Lucas— standing at the bar, sipping his beer. My eyes meet his for just a moment, and I swear I see the faintest hint of a smile on his lips as he watches me approach him.

Just as I'm about to close the last few feet of distance between us, a figure steps in front of me. A man with golden blonde hair and tattoos snaking up both of his muscular arms obstructs my view. He's at least six feet tall, forcing me to tilt my head back to make eye contact.

"Hey there, beautiful," he says, his voice tinged with enthusiasm. "I couldn't help but notice you from across the room. What's your name?" he asks. I can barely hear him over the music, but I catch the word "name."

It wouldn't hurt to give him my name.

"Rosie, how about you?"

His grin is wide, practically stretching from ear to ear. "Marcus. Mind if I buy you a drink?"

My eyes drift over to the bar, and as I do, Lucas's eyes are hard and glaring at the back of Marcus's head. He is no longer talking to his friends, or drinking his beer, he's completely motionless, watching our interaction.

"Thanks for the offer," I say, choosing my words carefully so as not to offend him. "I was actually just on my way to meet someone." I try not to slur my words, but I'm unsuccessful.

I attempt to move past him, and a warm, sweaty hand grabs onto my wrist, pulling me back. I gasp at the suddenness and intensity of it. My eyes fling to Lucas in panic as my chest hits Marcus's body.

Lucas doesn't hesitate.

He's off the chair in a second, his eyes glowing with pure rage.

"Get off me!" I yell, trying to break my arm away from his tight grasp. This isn't playful or flirty. This is dangerous.

"Come on, princess. Just come back with me and I'll show

you what a good night is," his disgusting, slurred voice says into my ear. I shiver at the thought, ripping myself out of his grasp and pushing myself away.

Marcus's eyes flash with anger, and his fists raise as if he wanted to hit me. Before he has the chance, Lucas smashes into his body, barrelling him into a group of people at the end of the bar. A few fall in the process and I rush to help them up, feeling awful that they've been caught in the middle of a fight, all because of me.

"I'm so sorry!" I shout to one of the girls who fell.

"Don't be! He's been a pig to us all night!" she shouts back, dusting off her tights.

I squeeze her shoulder in appreciation and turn to Lucas. He's on the floor, wrestling with Marcus. I can see blood on Lucas's lip.

By now, the entire club has stopped dancing and is watching Lucas and Marcus with a mixture of emotions. Some are covering their mouths in shock and others are cheering them on. Meanwhile, Lucas's friends are trying to pull him off Marcus.

I can see Elijah is trying to squeeze past the shocked spectators, his eyes asking me if I'm okay. I nod, looking around for Maddy and Sophia, but I can't see them. I'll have to find them once I know Lucas is okay.

Lucas tries to go for Marcus again despite his friends and Elijah holding them both back, but I grab his wrist, pulling him back.

"Stop!" I shout.

Lucas doesn't look at me but continues to gut Marcus with his eyes. His arm is tense, and I can feel his veins beneath his skin as he clenches his fist. His back is hunched over—ready for a fight.

Marcus wipes his bloodied lip and cut cheekbone, glaring at Lucas with such hate, the air grows colder around us. Before either man can go for each other again, a security guard pushes through the crowd, ordering us to get out.

I keep my hand on Lucas's wrist, firmly, until we're outside of the club. Lucas's friends and Elijah follow us out—walking behind Lucas and I.

"Are you okay?" Lucas asks, his voice gentle. I nod, unable to speak.

He gently picks up my wrist and inspects it for any damage. "I'm fine," I say, my voice coming out breathy and shaking.

"That son of a bitch," Lucas mutters, his voice a low grumble. I look down at my arm, and see a small, red mark on my wrist.

"It's nothing, Lucas. It would've been much worse if you hadn't been there," I reassure him, rubbing my wrist.

"It's not fine. No woman should be treated like that."

Before I can say anything, Marcus walks out of the door, still being escorted by security. Lucas storms towards him and chaos breaks out again.

"Lucas, stop!" I yell.

"I'll call the police!" the security guard yells, pulling Marcus behind him.

"Lucas, this won't solve anything! You've hit him once, that's enough," Elijah says, pulling on Lucas's arm, stopping him in his tracks.

"Come on then, you want to hit me again? All for that uptight, little bitch?" Marcus spits in my direction, and usually that would upset me, but I'm too focused on making sure Lucas doesn't go to prison.

"Lucas, stop!" I say again, putting myself in his tracks. I push his chest hard, running out of options.

"Look at me!" I shout, pushing him again. His breathing is hard, and his eyes stay on Marcus who is still hurling insults at me. I ignore him, his slurred voice mixing into background noise, and all I can hear is Lucas's hard, harsh breathing.

"Look at me!" I shout again, louder. I push his chest again, moving him further away from Marcus. Lucas's eyes meet mine.

"I'm fine. He's not worth a criminal charge."

"You're right," he says, rubbing his face with his bloodied hand. Elijah runs back into the club, and I hope he's running to grab Sophia and Maddy—I can't leave without them.

"You okay, man?" one of his friends asks.

"Yeah, thanks, Chris." He gently slaps Chris's shoulder in thanks.

Chris turns to me. "What about you? Are you okay?" he asks, his eyes full of real concern. My heart softens at this strange man being concerned and worried for me.

"I'm okay, thank you. I'm Rosie, by the way." I hold my hand out for him to shake, and he takes it with a friendly smile on his face.

"It's nice to meet you, I'm Chris." He looks behind him at Marcus, still shouting a load of bull. "You can shut up and piss off!" he orders. He ignores Marcus's "clever" comeback and leads Lucas and I out into the car park adjacent to the club.

"Wait! Maddy, Sophia and Elijah are somewhere here. I can't leave without them," I explain, stopping in my tracks and turning to scan the leaving crowd.

As I do, Elijah comes out of the club, walking with Maddy and Sophia. Relief floods me. One by one, they join us at the entrance to the car park, laughing and joking about what just happened.

"I cannot believe you actually hit the guy!" Maddy laughs, kissing Sophia on the forehead. "I feel like I'm in school again! What a wild night, wow!"

Lucas chuckles, and I struggle to find something to say. My brain is still foggy from the alcohol, and I now just want my bed.

Maddy's eyes flash with an idea.

"You should ask him to be your plus one for our wedding!" she says, looking straight at Lucas.

Lucas opens his mouth to speak, but I interrupt him, not wanting him to tell them he's already asked.

I shoot her a look. "Maddy, you're really drunk. Maybe someone should take you home?" I suggest, hoping Lucas doesn't have any ideas.

"Come on, Maddy. Let's go!" Sophia encourages, urging her with her eyes.

Maddy gently shrugs her off. "Rosie hasn't got a date to the wedding, and she's stressing about it. Will you go with her? I'm officially inviting you," she says, her smile bigger than the Grand Canyon.

Is she for real?

"Maddy, stop. I'm perfectly capable of finding my own dates. I'm a grown woman, for God's sake," I snap, feeling my face flush and my stomach drop in utter humiliation. Maddy's face drops, and she frowns. Her mouth opens but before she can say another word, I lift my hand, silencing her. "I'm going to go home. I'm tired. I'll see you all later," I say, wishing I can crawl in a hole and hide away forever.

I wave to everyone, and I start to walk down the street.

"Woah, we're not leaving you. We're going to take you home,"

Sophia insists.

"I'm fine. I don't live too far away. You guys go, it's late," I instruct, not wanting to take them out of their way.

"I live next door, so I can walk with you," Lucas offers. For a moment, I completely forgot that Lucas lives next door to me. I blink, but don't see why that will be an issue.

"Did you walk here, too?" I ask, not wanting to admit I'll feel safer with Lucas. After all, he did take and give one hell of a beating for me, today.

"I walked from the office. I'm happy to walk with you."

Chapter Twelve

Once we say our goodbyes and make sure our friends get into their taxis safely, Lucas and I start our walk back to our flat.

Now that we're alone, things feels different. I feel awkard, and I'm not sure what to say.

"I'm sorry about them," I say, feeling humiliated by what happened tonight.

"There's nothing to apologise for," he says, strolling casually with his hands in his pockets. Occasionally, our arms brush, and I have to physically remind myself to keep a distance between us. Otherwise, I drift towards him.

For now, I'm blaming it on the alcohol.

Before I can say anything else, I lose my footing and slip off the curb. Lucas quickly grabs my waist, pulling me up before I hit the cold, wet concrete. I cry out as my ankle twists, and I grab hold of Lucas's shoulders, trying to balance myself.

"Are you okay?" he asks, concern filling his gorgeous features as he looks down at me in his arms.

"What's with you and being the hero today?" I ask, trying to deflect from the fact I've embarrassed myself … again.

"It is becoming a regular occurrence," he says, grinning. A single piece of hair falls near his eye, and in my drunken haze, I reach out and tug it behind his ear.

Biting my lip, I pull my hand away as I realise what I'm doing.

"I'm sorry," I mutter, not sure what is coming over me. One moment I hate him, the next I want to jump his bones. It's confusing and conflicting, and deep down, I like it.

"You have nothing to apologise for," he says, his voice a mere whisper. His soft breath falls on my face, and I almost gasp at how intimate it feels.

"How's your ankle?" he asks, adjusting us so I'm sitting on the curb beside him. I almost pout when he's no longer touching me, but I manage to stop myself. Before he asked, I barely even noticed the throbbing pain erupting in my ankle.

I wince, touching the touch of my ankle, hoping to reduce the searing pain.

"I'm going to take that as not being okay," he says, offering his arm. I take it, not wanting to be proud at this moment.

"Come on, I'll take you home. Just grab onto my arm," he says, the lust and passion completely gone from his voice.

"Thank you," I say as I grab onto his arm, struggling to pull myself up from the wet floor. Once we manage it, Lucas gestures for me to climb onto his back.

I scoff. "Uh, no way in hell," I say, hobbling on the side of the road.

He rolls his eyes. "We're about ten minutes from the flat, and if you hobble like this, it'll take us thirty. Just climb on my back," he says, gesturing again.

I look around, hoping no one's around.

Lucas sighs, rolling his eyes. "Rosie, get on my back. No one is around," he says, his voice half-reassuring, and half-annoyed.

"Fine, but you better walk quickly," I snap, mumbling curses under my breath as I get into position.

"I was planning on taking a leisurely stroll with someone on my back," he says, sarcasm dripping from his mouth. One minute I want him to kiss me, and the next, I can't imagine a worse way to die.

I attempt to jump on his back, but with my ankle throbbing, it's proving to be difficult.

"Rosie. Just jump on," he says, impatience feeding its way through his tone.

"Shut up and stop rushing me!" I pause, wrapping my injured leg around his thigh. I try to clamber onto his back by pulling his shoulders, but I can't get up.

"Oh, for the love of all that's holy!" Lucas turns around and pulls me into his arms.

I squeal as he sweeps me up, huffing as he takes my weight.

"Lucas, put me down!" I struggle in his arms, not wanting to be like this for ten whole minutes.

He ignores me and starts walking down the street towards our flats.

"Lucas, I mean it!" I snap, embarrassment filling me as I become trapped in his strong, muscled arms.

Part of me loves it, but the stronger part of me hates it.

"And I'm a tired, tipsy man, who just wants his bed," he says, continuing his long strides. I keep struggling, trying to wriggle out of his arms. I'd rather hobble for thirty minutes than be stuck like this.

"Stop it, or I'll drop you!" he protests, holding me tighter to his chest.

"Drop me then! Anything is better than this," I say.

"Really? You'd rather be in pain than just accept some help?" he asks, shaking his head. He still doesn't slow down as my protests continue.

"Yes! I'm a proud woman, and I'm being manhandled!" I say, louder than he probably would have liked.

"You'd know if I were manhandling you, and be quiet! I don't want people getting the wrong idea," he says, shushing me.

"Trust me, I don't want you manhandling me," I say, grimacing at the thought. Little does he know, I may have thought about it once or twice, but right now, it's off the cards.

He chuckles, "Like I've said before, our walls are thin, so I know more than you let on," he says.

"You are disgusting," I say, trying to hide the smile on my face before Lucas sees. Lucas has a way of making me laugh, and it's starting to feel dangerous as my heart starts to beat a little faster. He continues to walk down the street, holding me in his arms as he whistles a song. We stay like this for a few minutes as I succumb to this torment.

After ten minutes, Lucas shifts me and I'm carefully being lowered back onto my feet.

"See? Didn't take that long, did it?" he asks, pointing towards my flat door.

I huff, searching for my keys in my bag. "Well, I'd like to say this was a pleasure, but as usual, you've managed to repulse me," I say.

Lucas chuckles and grabs my bag.

"Hey! First you manhandle me, and now you're robbing me? So much for being a gentleman!" I gasp. Lucas rolls his eyes but doesn't respond. Instead, he pulls out my keys and opens my flat door.

"You're going to get me in trouble one day," he says, holding back a smile.

I smirk and hobble into my flat, enjoying being back.

"Thanks for getting me home," I say, truly meaning it.

He nods briefly before he unlocks his flat door.

"Try to keep the noise down tonight, eh?" he says, winking before he disappears into his flat, shutting the door.

"Pig!" I shout, slamming my own door.

I lean against the cool wood and take a deep breath as I try to calm my beating heart. I can't stop the small smile that appears on my mouth at the thought of tonight, and I already know I'm going to get hurt.

Chapter Thirteen

"What cover do you think we should go for?" Rachel asks, swivelling in my chair and attempting to hold up three different cover designs, as I pace up and down the room. Rachel has almost finished the first draft of the book.

"That's not really on my mind right now."

"It should be on your mind. A promotion at work is a lot more important than revealing you have no date to your family," she says, sighing and placing the cover designs down.

"You don't have my family. It doesn't matter that I've made a successful life for myself. It doesn't matter that I'm happy, and I'm a full-grown adult. All they want is for me to be married, and to have babies. I just don't know how to win," I say, truly feeling deflated.

"You do have an option," Rachel suggests, looking at me like I know what she's talking about.

"I'm all ears!" I say, keeping my eyes to the floor, wanting to avoid the calendar which now shows the big red cross, signalling the wedding is near. It feels like I'm trying to grab water. It's all just falling out of my fingers.

"Come on, you know exactly who I'm talking about," she huffs, chucking her chunky notebook down on my desk.

I look at her in disbelief. "No, you can't be serious," I say, stopping in my tracks completely.

"Well, what else do you suggest? You can still go on your dates and find 'the one' but take Lucas to the wedding." I now regret texting Rachel about what Maddy said the other night in my tipsy rage. I didn't know she would back her up.

"And how does that help me with the promotion?" I ask, desperately trying to find an excuse out of this nightmare. I can't imagine spending all of that time with Lucas, *and* my family.

I shudder at the thought.

"The promotion deadline isn't for another month or so after the wedding. Figure that out then. Plus, we're in the final stages of the book, and we've already started promoting it. My stats have gone up, so we just need to find a few promoters," she says, still looking between the cover design photos.

"I'll contact a few people I know," I say, already pulling a few contacts from my emails.

She picks up the cover designs and heads towards the door.

"I like the second one," I say, not looking up from my computer.

"I totally agree. I'll let the cover designer know!" she says. I can hear the smirk in her voice, and that gives me five hours of uninterrupted, girl-boss motivation.

Ring, ring.

I jump out of the world's perfect workflow. Maybe it's not that important, and I can get back to emailing news outlets and bloggers. I let the phone go to voicemail and continue with my groundbreaking work. I can't remember a time I've felt so energised and inspired, and I didn't want to waste it.

Ring, ring.

I pick up my phone, which is causally lying on the desk, with a huff. I frown at the unknown caller ID, wondering if I should even answer it. "Hello?" I ask, warily, but still professional.

"Rosie?" a husky voice asks, the sound of banging is in the distance.

"Depends on who is calling," I say, not about to be scammed by some notorious scammer. That's happened before, and I'll be damned if I let it happen again.

"It's Lucas."

My heart stops and all the moisture in my mouth seems to evaporate at the sound of his name.

"How did you get my number?" I ask. "And why are you calling me?"

"If you let me explain, I will," he says, humour laced in his words.

I sigh, "Quickly."

"I got your number from Elijah when I went to grab my daily, morning coffee."

"Okay? Good for you, I guess." I don't see the point of this conversation. If anything, he's wasting valuable time. Time I could be out winning *my* promotion.

"As I'm paying, I realised I left my work bag in my flat, so I went back to grab it."

I hold the bridge of my nose, quickly losing my patience. "If you don't have anything important to say, I'm afraid I must cut this conversation short. Unlike you, I am really busy," I say, about to hang up.

"I think your flat is flooding."

"What?" I exclaim.

"I think your apartmen—"

I cut him off. "I heard you the first time! Why didn't you lead with that? And why didn't you do something!" I pick up my bag, shoving random things inside, wasting no time rushing down to my flat to make sure the whole thing isn't a lake by the time I finish tonight. With my throbbing ankle, I don't make it very far before I take my shoes off and chuck them in my bag.

"Should I kick your door down? I wanted to ask—"

"Yes! Yes, kick it down! Do you see water? Did you call the landlord?" I ask, pausing in the doorway, my heart threatening to give out on me any second.

"There's water because it's leaking into my flat. And yes, the landlord is on his way," he says, sarcasm thick in his husky, deep voice.

I roll my eyes. "Then bust down the door! Do whatever you have to do to stop the water. I'm on my way," I say, already outside of the office. Knowing I have no time to walk or run back to my flat with my ankle, I signal a taxi, hoping they can get me there in less than five minutes.

Finally, a taxi takes mercy on me and stops. I don't hesitate to jump in, shouting out my directions and telling them my flat is soon to be the Pacific Ocean. He says nothing and looks at me as if I've grown six heads.

"Come on!" I say, hating that I sound so pushy, but my flat depends on it. I can't have a failing love life, the possibility of losing my dream promotion, *and* a flooded flat all in the space of a few weeks. Not happening.

He finally starts driving and I decide to add Lucas's number to my contacts. I'm not surprised we haven't swapped numbers before since Lucas is rude. I also don't see Lucas as a texting kind of guy.

Once the taxi driver pulls up to my flat, I quickly transfer him the money and I jump out without another word. I race up the stairs, knowing the elevator will take too long. Before I know it, I'm standing in front of my smashed flat door and a very shirtless Lucas.

"Oh my God," I say as I tiptoe on the wet floor. Lucas looks up and pushes his hair out of his face, getting up from the floor.

"What the hell happened?" I ask, looking around at the damage. It wasn't terrible, but it wasn't liveable now.

Oh God, what am I going to do?

"I'm not a plumber, but I'm certain the water is coming from your bathroom. I've turned the water off until the plumber can arrive," he says, his hands on his bare hips.

"The bathroom sink," I say, finally realising the leak under my bathroom sink is the culprit. I sit down on the arm of my sofa and put my head in my hands. "I should've just called the damn plumber," I say into my hands.

I can hear Lucas walking towards me by the splash of his feet, and I don't stop him. In fact, if he wasn't here, this would've been a lot worse.

"Thank you, Lucas. If you weren't here, I—"

He interrupts me by placing his hand on my shoulder. "You don't have to thank me. Anyone would've done it," he says, squeezing my shoulder gently. I give him a small smile. "Plus, your water was ruining my flat too. I hate redecorating so it was also in my best interest to stop the flood," he says.

I laugh, kicking some water at him before looking at my

ruined floors.

"Oh God, just look at the mess!" I exclaim. I get up and look around to see if there's anything important on the floor. Luckily for me, I keep everything important backed up and up high.

There is a knock on the open door.

"You guys call for a plumber?" a man, in his late forties asks. I want to yell and shout and take my anger and frustration out on him.

Is that a joke, or is he so used to seeing burst pipes and floods of water where water shouldn't be, that he generally can't see that my favourite shoes are covered in freezing cold water?

Lucas glances at me, and I'm sure he's seen the rage threatening to explode. "Yeah, I think the pipe in her bathroom has burst," Lucas says, taking the lead.

The plumber goes into the bathroom, Lucas hot on his tail. In a moment of weakness, I find myself staring after Lucas. His back muscles are taunt, and his shoulders are so broad, I can't imagine ever wrapping my arms fully around them.

"You coming?" Lucas asks, and I realise he's looking at me and the only way he would've missed me checking him out, is if he's blind. Fabulous. Today really can't get much better.

"Yeah, I'll be in now. I just have to make some calls. See if anyone can take me in for a few days," I say, grabbing my phone knowing this is the best way for me to use my time.

"Okay, we'll be in the death trap you call a bathroom," he says, trying to joke with me. I manage a small smile, but I don't have much more energy left in me.

He heads into the bathroom, and I realise that the first time he's seeing this flat, it's an actual mess. And not the mess our parents are worried about when they're having guests over.

An actual, damp, awful, and expensive mess.

I can just hear the jokes he's going to make after this is all over.

I call everyone in my contact lists, and not one person says I can stay with them.

Rachel is travelling to New York with her editor, so I haven't bothered calling her, Madilyn is still fixing her relationship with Sophia, and Elijah is currently sharing his bed with a man he met a few nights ago. Everyone else just gives me a bunch of different excuses.

The plumber and Lucas come out, and I'm at a loss of what I can do. I stand, waiting for the verdict.

"I can fix the pipe," the plumber says. I wait before I celebrate as there sounds like a big "but" is coming.

"But"—*there it is*—"I haven't got the part with me. I'll have to order it in, so I won't be able to fix it until Monday."

Monday? *Monday*? That's an entire three days away!

"Isn't there something you can do? Surely there's a fast-track service when there's an emergency like this?" I ask, hoping and praying this isn't it. Where am I going to live until then?

"I'm sorry, but that's the latest. Have you got anywhere to stay in the meantime?"

"I'll figure something out."

"Why don't you stay with me? I only live next door, and this means you can come in and grab anything you need," Lucas offers. I'm at a loss for words, and I can't believe I'm considering it.

Now, he's my best option, and he's right. It's convenient.

"If you're sure that's okay?" I ask, embarrassed that my life has truly come to this.

"Of course. I want to help in any way I can. I'll take the sofa, it's no problem for me."

"Thank you," I say.

I really don't have many options. Plus, it'll only be for a few days. I can hold on for a few days.

Right?

Chapter Fourteen

I place the few possessions I have in my bag onto Lucas's dining room table and look around his flat. I'm immediately enveloped by the ambiance of Lucas's space. Dim, moody lighting casts shadows on walls full of abstract photography and articles which are framed in a black frame. The shelves are lined with vinyl records, classic literature, and a couple of vintage cameras. A shaggy rug lies beneath a coffee table that hosts a collection of journals. The room is tinged with deep hues—midnight blues, charcoal greys, and rustic browns.

The air is saturated with male cologne, entangled with the faintest hint of cedarwood. Despite the sophistication, I can see the lived-in comfort which stops this space from being too pretentious.

Lucas's flat is a huge contrast to my own space. It's like stepping into a different world, despite both spaces being next-door.

The flat is immaculate; There's no dust, no piles of clothes

in the corner of the room, and no stacked-up plates begging to
be cleaned by the sink. I'm not sure why I assumed his place
would be like a teenage boy's room, but I have to say, I'm very
glad I'm wrong. The only thing out of place are pieces of paper
in the middle of his table and some photos hung up of recent
news articles and reports.

He notices me looking at them, and steps forward, into my
line of vision.

I blink. "What's that?" I ask, hoping I'm not prying too much.
But, if we're to live together for a few days, I think getting to
know each other is important. After all, who casually hangs
up news reports and papers? Serial killers and people who
only go shopping at night.

"What do you think it is?" he asks, raising his eyebrows in a
challenge.

I cross my arms over my chest. "Okay, Mr. Sarcastic."

As Lucas carefully lines up his shoes by the door, I find
myself drawn to the articles hanging on the wall, each of
them bearing his name. The headlines vary from gripping
investigative pieces to heart-warming human interest stories,
showcasing the versatility of his writing skills. Just looking at
the headlines I can see he really cares about what he writes.

"So these are for work?" I ask, turning my attention back to
him. There's a genuine curiosity in my voice as I truly want to
know.

He nods, his eyes meeting mine with a hint of shyness. "Yeah,"
he responds modestly. "I've been working as a journalist for a
few years now. I'm also hoping to start up my own journalism
school someday."

My admiration for him deepens. "Wow, that's very impressive," I remark, with genuine admiration in my voice. "Starting

your own journalism school is a fantastic dream."

Lucas smiles, his face lighting up with enthusiasm. "Thank you, Rosie. It's something I'm really passionate about. I believe in the power of storytelling and I think I could teach others. I want more feeling in articles, instead of just pointless gossip."

My gaze remains fixed on the articles which are lined up on the wall with new appreciation for him. I'm really seeing him through new eyes, and I'm scared of how it's making me feel.

I continue looking around his flat. "Where should I put my stuff?" I ask, looking around for some space.

"It's a one bedroom, so you take the room, I'll take the sofa. I'll empty a drawer for you," he offers.

"I don't know. I'm all about equality, and it's your place. I'll take the sofa and I'll feel less guilty about it," I insist, not wanting to take this man's bed from him.

"I insist," he says, walking into his room. His flat is almost identical to mine, minus my taste and unique furniture.

Lucas comes out with an armful of bedding and puts them into the washing machine.

"Don't worry, we'll have these washed and dried by the time you sleep," he promises, adding fabric softener into the load. I'm not sure if it's the fact he's doing laundry *and* using fabric softener, or it's the fact he's being so nice and welcoming that's making me watch him in awe. It's like we're strangers, meeting for the first time. I hardly blink, not wanting to miss a thing.

"Do you want something to eat?" he asks, opening one of his cupboards, and rummaging through to find something.

I don't realise how hungry I am until he mentions food. I hold my stomach, feeling the vibrations of my grumbling stomach beneath my hand.

"I've got some pasta?" he says, though it sounds more like

a question, glancing over at me. I nod, not really caring what we have. After the events of today, I can eat a whole village. That's always been my problem. When I'm stressed and tired, I eat. When I'm happy and excited, I feel nauseous. Most people are the opposite, but the way I see it, when you're stressed and you feel like the whole world is crumbling on top of you, you need energy just to be able to cope.

"Not going to lie, I always ruin pasta," he reveals, a grin forming on his face.

"Well, lucky for you, I'm the master at making pasta. It's one of my favourite dishes."

I walk over to him and take the lead. "Where are your pans?" I ask, not wanting to search through his drawers and cupboards.

He points towards the cupboard under the sink. I grab a saucepan and add the water and salt and add it to the stove. I attempt to turn on the hob, but it's one of those new induction hobs I haven't had the pleasure of buying yet.

I press different buttons, hoping one of them will work.

"Need help?" he asks from behind me. I jump slightly but manage to keep my cool.

"I'm sure I'll—"

He interrupts me by reaching around me, his forearm gently grazing my shoulder, and holds down the biggest button until it flashes.

"Now you press the plus sign until you get to the number nine," he says, his breath brushing against my neck. I know he is only trying to help, and he's not doing it in a seductive way, but I can't help but shiver. I haven't been this close to a man since Gabe, and ever since, I've felt wired. I manage to untangle myself from him.

"Where do you keep your pasta?" I ask, wondering if it'll be obvious if I ask to open his kitchen window.

"Uh, I'll grab it," he says, scratching his chin and pulling away from me. He pulls out a blue packet of pasta and puts it on the side.

"How come you can't make pasta?" I ask, distracting myself with small talk. This kitchen seems awfully small right now.

"You know when you cook pasta, it goes soft?" he asks, looking at the bag of dry pasta.

I nod, not sure where he's going with this, or how it's relevant to my question.

"I manage to make it harder than before it came out of that packet," he says, laughing at his own expense.

"Oh God, that's tragic!" I exclaim, covering my mouth with my hand, still in hysterics. "And you're a grown man?"

"Yeah, well not everyone can be a chef!" he protests, laughing.

"You don't have to be a chef to cook pasta," I say, tutting and shaking my head.

"Come on, I'm starving. I've been kicking down doors all day!"

We both focus on cooking the pasta, and by the time we're done, it's eight o'clock and I can feel my eyes becoming heavy.

We sit on the sofa, side by side, with our bowls of pasta. Lucas puts the TV on and we sit in peaceful quiet, eating our food and watching some crappy late-night show.

I find myself looking at Lucas out of the corner of my eye, studying the stranger beside me. It seems like forever ago since I last sat down with someone and ate a proper meal with them in front of the TV.

It's nice—really nice.

I also hadn't expected to be with Lucas right now. I had

barely spoken to him up until a few weeks ago.

Once we finish our pasta, I take both of our plates to the kitchen to clean up.

"No, you're a guest. I can't have you cook me pasta and clean. Sit down, I'll be right out," he says, ordering me out of the kitchen.

This Lucas is different from the Lucas I thought I knew. Maybe I didn't give him enough of a chance.

Before Lucas fills the bowl up with water to wash up, he takes the now-clean bedding out of the washing machine, and places them into the dryer. I watch him from the corner of my eye, scared I will miss something. He then fills up the bowl, and starts washing up.

I feel bad standing here doing nothing.

I pick up a plate he's just washed and placed on the drying rack, and start to dry it with a dish towel. "No, I want to help. After all, you have literally saved my life. I'd be homeless if it wasn't for you." As I say it, I realise how incredibly dramatic that sounds. I have money, so I would just rent out a hotel, but there were no openings close to the office. "I don't mean homeless, homeless. I'd just be a bit stuck," I say. He raises his eyebrows and smirks as I bumble my way through like an idiot. Why am I making this so awkward?

And, of course, I decide to make it even more awkward.

"So, I see a lot of women passing through here. Will any of them mind that I'm here?" I ask, staring intently at the plate I'm currently drying..

Lucas coughs. "I'm not sure what you're implying."

"You know, any potential girlfriends who will be annoyed that I'm here?" I ask, thinking it's important to know. If I'm dating someone, I'd want to know another woman was staying with my boyfriend. It's just law.

"I don't have a lot of women here," he defends, scoffing and handing me another plate, still dodging the question.

"As long as you don't have a girlfriend or wife, then we're all good!" I exclaim, placing the now, very dry plate on the counter.

"I don't." He pauses and looks at me. "What about you? I'm not going to be happy if another man comes here and punches me in the face."

Breathing a subtle sigh, I pick up another plate. "I'm single."

As I say it, I can feel myself tense up, waiting for the judge-y comment about my time running out or a question asking how I'm single and for how long.

"What's your favourite film?" he asks, completely catching me off guard. I raise my eyebrows at him, confused at this sudden change of topic. He doesn't look at me as he puts cutlery away, the clanging of metal drowning out the silence.

I decide not to question it.

This is his way of showing me respect.

"I know it's going to sound ridiculous"— I pause, chewing the inside of my cheek—"but it's *Legally Blonde*." I say it quickly, shutting my eyes in embarrassment.

Lucas raises his eyebrows, a smirk threatening to break out from his lip.

"It's the first film I watched that showed me that I could do anything. I was destined to work in the family restaurant, and I didn't want to. I felt like my life was on the wrong track, but the pressure was forcing me to stay on." Lucas gently places cutlery down and leans on the counter, giving me his full attention, completely serious.

I continue, scared to lose my nerve. "I was sixteen and I

was at my cousin's house, studying for exams—exams I didn't think I needed. They felt like a waste of time. Why would I try and pass these tests when I knew it wouldn't get me anywhere?" Lucas remains quiet, truly invested in the story. "Maddy turned on the TV, trying to cheer me up and distract me from my impending crappy life with no prospects or hope," I hear Lucas snicker. My eyes shoot to his, his face becoming serious again. Rolling my eyes, I continue. "Anyway, *Legally Blonde* was on. I'd heard of it, but I'd never watched it in its entirety. The next day, I was researching marketing degrees."

I look at Lucas, shocked to see him trying to hide a smile.

"What?" I snap, embarrassed that I just opened up to someone, and they're laughing at me.

"No, nothing," he says, shaking his head and scratching his chin, trying to hide the smile I can obviously still see.

"No, come on. If you have something to say," I prompt, arching my eyebrow.

"Isn't *Legally Blonde* about a lawyer? Not a marketer?" he asks.

"Yes. I didn't mean I wanted to do exactly what she did. It was the idea that a woman just changed her life. She made it happen, and it inspired me, that's why I love that film," I explain, leaning against his counter. As I do, a plate shatters under my elbow and a searing pain slices through my arm.

"Oh, fuck!" I screech, holding my bleeding arm to my chest and squeezing my eyes tightly shut. This cannot be happening right now...

"Bloody hell, Rosie! Are you okay? Lucas asks, storming towards me, his eyes dark and menacing as he stares at my hand, clutched on my elbow, trying to keep the red liquid, which should remain in my body, from dripping out onto his clean, kitchen floor.

"I'm fine, nothing I haven't done before," I try to say before he interrupts.

"You've got to be more careful," he snaps. I stand straighter, not liking his arsey tone.

"Stop being so condescending. Accidents happen, okay?" I snap back. His eyes flash with a streak of annoyance which I'm quickly becoming familiar with, like I'm a bug at the bottom of his shoe. I remember why he's not my favourite person in the entire world.

As he's standing there, watching me, my anger turns into something else. I can feel my heart beating and my palms start to sweat.

"And who is the fully grown 'adult' who flooded her flat and cut herself on some glass, and twisted her ankle?" he asks, chuckling to himself. The guy isn't wrong. What makes it worse is that he has no idea that the mess he can see is not as bad as the rest of my life. I still have no date to the wedding, and I am barely holding on to that promotion.

"Excuse me? I inquire, completely over this hot and cold attitude.

He says nothing, except take one step closer to me. I step back, backing into the counter again. I'm careful not to touch the glass, but that's the least of my worries.

He tears his eyes away from my bleeding arm and meets mine, his eyes hazy and dilated.

I quickly turn away from him, and seek the sink, not trusting my emotions. I feel hot and bothered, and I'm scared I'll embarrass myself.

I run the cold tap.

I place my arm under the running tap, gasping as the water

briefly stings, but relief soon floods in as the water soothes my burning skin, cleaning the wound I have just carelessly received. My eyes shut at the feeling, everything in my mind is quiet for a few seconds, and I greedily accept it.

I can hear movement and rustling as something is opened behind me, but I fight the urge to look. I relish in the cold water's embrace.

"Here, let me wrap that," Lucas says, his voice a mere whisper as he lightly caresses my shoulder, encouraging me to turn around.

His voice slams me back into reality. I sigh as the noise in my head comes crashing back in.

I don't resist Lucas's attempts to wrap my arm. As I observe Lucas, I notice he's shocked that I don't argue with him. He looks shocked that I'm making this easier than he thought I would. His eyes stay firmly planted on my arm, and for some reason, I feel a pang of disappointment which sinks into my stomach.

"Well, I can confirm that I don't think it's fatal," he jokes, a small smirk on his soft, pink lips.

"So, you're telling me, I might not lose the arm?" I ask, feigning fake enthusiasm.

"You're correct. Congratulations," he praises, chucking the bloody gauze in the kitchen bin beside us. A small laugh slips from my parted lips, soon followed by a deep, chuckle from Lucas.

"I think I'm going to turn in for the night. I have work in the morning," I say, suddenly feeling the day's activities.

"That's true, I don't pin you as the type of woman who likes to be late," he says, leaning against the counter.

"And what kind of woman would you pin me as?" I ask, the

130

thought of sleep is now the last thing on my mind.

Lucas is different. I'm not sure if it's good or bad yet, but I'm working on it. I'll have him figured out soon enough, and when I do, he won't be able to surprise me. I hate surprises.

His mouth pouts as he ponders the question. Too many seconds go by, and I'm left impatient.

"Well? Have I succeeded in making *you* speechless?" I ask, taking great pleasure in seeing him stunned for words. A journalist, no less. The occupation literally requires you to figure people out. The good, the bad, and the incredibly ugly, and yet he's struggling to figure me out.

"No, I'm just pondering," he says, looking me up and down. I smirk, knowing he has nothing. He has no idea what kind of woman I am, and that pleases me. Perhaps when he figured me out, he won't be as interested or intrigued. I'm just a woman who can't hold down a man, and I'm almost thirty. There's nothing exciting or compelling about me.

"Goodnight, Lucas," I say, walking out of the kitchen. Lucas clears his throat and I stop, waiting for whatever stupid comment is going to come out of his mouth.

"Don't you need bedding?" he asks, pointing towards the dryer.

I bite my lip. "How long before it's done?" I ask, my eyes feeling tired suddenly.

Lucas opens the dryer's doors and places his hand in, feeling the sheets. His face is scrunched in concentration, and I can't help but smile briefly.

"I think it's all done!" he declares, pulling the sheets out of the dryer.

"Here, let me," I offer, not liking the idea of someone else doing something I am more than capable of doing myself.

I follow Lucas into his bedroom and hope I don't listen to the thoughts in my head.

Chapter Fifteen

T he room is spotless.
I'm not sure what I expected from his room, but it isn't this.

The feel of Lucas in this room with me is making me feel strange. I've spent the last few years hearing everything that goes on in here, and I'm having a hard time distracting myself when he's standing beside me, smelling so good.

I continue to look around the room, unsure of what to do next.

"Are you just going to stand there while I make the bed, I'm letting you stay in?" Lucas asks, a smirk pulling at his lips, leaning against the door watching me.

"Okay, calm down," I joke. He laughs, still standing there, watching me. I can feel the weight of his eyes on me as I try to focus on anything else. I get to work on the duvet cover, resisting the urge to look at him.

He says nothing but walks over and picks up a pillow and a pillowcase. We find ourselves on opposite sides of the bed and as I pull the duvet cover over the bed, my fingers brush against Lucas's. It's a fleeting touch, but it sends a shiver down my spine. I dare a glance in his direction, meeting his eyes for a brief moment. There's a warmth in his gaze as a smile tugs at the corners of his lips. I can't help but return the smile.

With each corner of the bed neatly tucked, we stand back to admire our handiwork. The bed is impeccably made and as we step away from the bed, I can't help but steal one last glance at Lucas. Our eyes meet once more, and this time, we don't smile as we look at each other, as if, for the first time.

Before long, Lucas leaves to sleep on the sofa. I think about what just happened until my eyes dart open, and the sun is streaming through the window.

***

Now, sitting in Lucas's flat on a Sunday afternoon, I'm forced to feel the terrible binding rope of loneliness gripping my chest for the millionth time this year. It never used to bother me, but now I crave connection and companionship. I've also lost my flat, which was always my safe space.

As if on queue, my phone vibrates with a notification. Sighing, I open up the notification.

It's the online dating site.

I click on the profile of a guy named Eddie who has just matched with me—my first match in a few days—and I'm intrigued. Just as I read over his profile, a message pops up from Eddie.

Eddie_Speeches: *Hi, I can't help but notice how beautiful you are.*

I smile, that lonely feeling dissipating.

Rosiexx: *Well, that's very kind of you to say.*

I leave it there, unable to think of a single thing to say. I'm out of touch. Seriously.

Eddie_Speeches: *Would you be around to have a drink with me soon?*

Eddie's message hangs in the air, a tempting offer.

Loneliness has a way of clouding my judgement recently.

I hesitate for a moment, my fingers hovering over the keyboard as I consider Eddie's proposition. Part of me is willing to take the chance. After all, I have been craving companionship, and this could be an opportunity.

Who knows? This could be the man for me.

I don't want to get in the way of fate … I think I'll let fate decide.

Rosiexx: *I'd love to meet up for a drink sometime.*

As I hit send, a mixture of anticipation and nervousness washes over me.

Eddie_Speeches: *That's great! How about tomorrow at The Brewery Lantern? Say, 7 PM?*

I pause, considering his offer.

Rosiexx: *Friday at 7 PM at The Brewery Lantern works for me. Looking forward to it.*

I set my phone aside with the feeling of excitement I haven't felt since I kissed Lucas.

****

The sun is setting, casting a warm, golden glow over the outdoor café where I agreed to meet my date, Eddie. The only reason I said yes to going on a date with him is because I was lonely and a little desperate for companionship—and maybe to forget about Lucas.

Now, as I sit here waiting, I can't help but feel a growing sense of unease. Perhaps I should have vetted him a bit more, or waited a little longer than a day of talking to agree to go out with him. Especially as I have an awful growing track record with men.

He told me to meet him at a quaint little coffee shop, which is only a fifteen minute walk from my flat. However, I've never come in here before because it usually hosts a lot of poetry readings and other niche events. Surely that isn't what he has in mind for a date?

I look around, becoming increasingly more worried about what I've signed myself up for. The atmosphere is teeming with unshaven men in turtle-necks and women carrying books and wearing oversized glasses.

It's not my scene, and the longer I stay sitting in this plaid armchair, the more tempted I am to leave. The one thing stopping me; I don't have the heart to stand someone up the way I was stood up.

There is an undeniable scent of brewing coffee mixing with existential despair.

Before I can turn my nose up any more, a guy who looks like Eddie's profile picture walks into the cafe. His attire is a blend of cosy comfort and a distinct nerdiness. He's draped in a knitted jumper that could have been handcrafted by a grandparent, he sports khaki trousers that seem plucked straight from a vintage clothing store, and his glasses look like something from Harry Potter.

Eddie notices me, and walks over and gives me a hug whilst I'm still sitting in the chair. It is an awkward fumbling action with tangled arms and his hair going up my nose.

"I'm Eddie, you must be Rosie?" he asks, taking a seat beside me in the other plaid armchair with rips on the arms.

I nod, and before I can say anything, he interrupts.

"You're going to love this. Nothing speaks to the soul like slam poetry."

As he says this, confirming my nightmare, I sag into my chair and feign a smile. "Yeah, sounds great."

As we sit there waiting for the first speaker, I try to start some conversation.

"So, you're an accountant?"

He barely looks at me as he nods. "Yeah. I've been doing this job for about six years now," he says, before looking back at his phone, not bothering to ask me a question.

"Do you enjoy it?" I ask, really trying to get something out of him.

He holds his hands up, shushing me as he leans forward in his chair, looking up at the stage. "The first poet is on," he says, his eyes barely giving me a second glance.

I roll my eyes, already regretting my decision of taking him up on his offer so soon. The speaker starts with a speech about how the government are the real enemies, their words punctuated by a guy banging a drum in the corner of the cafe.

"I totally relate to him," Eddie mutters. I try not to snicker, but the surrealness of this situation is getting to me. I hide the snicker as a cough, trying to focus on the words of the speaker, which makes me want to laugh more. Then, I watch as Eddie takes his phone. His thumbs are flying, typing out a message. I look down at his phone, wondering what he's typing so fast before I realise he's sending out a live tweet of the performance. I sink into my chair even further, trying not to laugh. I wasn't necessarily laughing at him. I'm pretty sure I'm laughing at the continuously bad situations I keep putting myself in. Surely you can't make these stories up?

Every so often, Eddie looks up and gives me a nod with a massive smile on his face as if to say, "Aren't we having a great time?" I smile back, giving him a half nod because I wasn't sure what else to do.

The next speaker starts reciting a piece that is basically an alphabetised grocery list but with unbelievably funny metaphors. "Apple … the influence of corrupt and sinful individuals." He breathes into the mic.

Once the speaker is at "Eggs," Eddie's phone sounds with a notification which is oddly familiar.

"Sorry, important work email," he whispers, though he's clearly just received a new match on the very same dating app we met on.

I take a sip of my coffee, keeping the smile on my face as this unfazed me. It's been crystal clear that we're not on the same page, since the moment he walked in. I'm not angry, just aware that my time could be better spent elsewhere. "No worries, Eddie. Work is important," I say, already thinking about how I'll find an excuse to leave.

The evening comes to an end and we step out into the night. "So, what did you think?" he asks, finally pocketing his phone as if he'd been fully present the entire time.

"It was … good," I say, holding back a laugh as I remember what I just sat through.

He looks at me, bewildered. "Just good? This is why I can't take women out on sophisticated dates. All they want is to be wined and dined, but what about us men? We also want that," he says, his face becoming increasingly red.

I can't hold back the laugh any longer as I realise what he's implying. "I would agreed with you if you actually asked me one question and wasn't on your phone, live tweeting the whole thing. Look, it's clear we are incredibly and painfully incompatible, so I'll be leaving. I hope you have a great rest of your night," I add, before turning on my heels and walking away.

****

As I walk towards Lucas's flat, I'm half-cringing and half-chuckling at the thought of Eddie. My pondering is cut short when my eyes catch sight of Lucas who is sitting on the steps outside of our flats beside a woman whose face I can't quite see.

In that split second, my heart sinks. Was it jealousy gnawing at me?

"Hey, Rosie," Lucas calls out, breaking me from my thoughts. The woman beside him looks up, giving me a warning look. As her eyes tell me to back away, I can feel a jolt of something inexplicable. Irritation? Anger?

"Hi," I respond, my voice straining as I narrow my eyes at the woman. "Looks like you're having a good night."

Lucas glances at the woman beside him and then back at me with a glint of something in his eyes. Is it regret? "Yeah, it's been interesting. Rosie, this is Delilah. Delilah, meet Rosie, my neighbour."

Neighbour?

I know this is a fact, but it feels … wrong, somehow.

Lucas's voice seems strained, the awkward tension vibrating off of him. Is he awkward because I'm there?

Delilah shoots me a displeased and distant smile. "Pleased to meet you."

I can hear the lack of enthusiasm and I don't want to stick around and feel unwelcome, especially if he's on a date.

My eyes meet Lucas's for a split second which ends up feeling like an eternity. I could have sworn there was a glint of something—longing? regret?—in his gaze.

"I'll be in shortly," Lucas says, his voice quiet as if he doesn't want Delilah hearing.

"Okay, see you in a bit," I say, wanting to get into the sanctuary of my flat, but I can't. I haven't been given the green light to move back in, so I'm stuck having to stay with Lucas and this palpable tension.

Lucas nods, his eyes trying to convey a message to me. "See you in a bit."

I can feel Lucas's eyes on my back, as well as Delilahs *pleasant* gaze. Once I'm inside his flat, I lean against the door behind me and exhale as I ponder the confusing mess of emotions I'm feeling—jealousy, yes, but also a yearning I haven't admitted to myself until recently. I'm also slapped in the face with reality—he doesn't like me like that, so why am I still pining over him?

I potter around the flat, trying to keep myself busy, but I can hear the muted conversation and laughter coming from outside. I resist the temptation to peek through the curtains, but I shake my head as if to dispel the thoughts.

Once Lucas's flat is insanely tidy, I stand in the living room, wondering what else I can do to distract myself.

Still hearing the muffled conversation, I quickly pick up a recent romance novel I've been reading. After reading one page, it makes me feel worse. I slam the book shut, frustrated that the fictional romance only makes me more aware of my non-existent love life, and the real-life situation happening just beyond my window. I toss the book onto the coffee table and turn on the TV, flipping through channel after channel, hoping to find something—*anything*—that can engage my attention.

I settle on re-watching my favourite comfort show, thinking maybe the familiarity will calm my nerves. But even my favourite show can't stop my mind from drifting back to Lucas and Delilah.

I switch off the TV, its chatter becoming nothing but irritating noise.

With a heavy sigh, I grab my headphones and chuck on workout gear I haven't worn in a year and decide on a different strategy. I scroll through my playlist and opt for some high-energy songs, hoping the beat can drown out both the external sounds and my own thoughts. As the music blasts in my ears, I start doing some exercises—jumping jacks, push-ups, and squats—in a desperate attempt to focus on physical exertion over emotional turmoil.

But halfway through my makeshift workout, I realise that no amount of physical activity can exhaust the emotional energy that's been building up inside me. The loneliness and longing is becoming too much; I can't stop thinking of Lucas.

Instead, I clean up and I head to bed. I can't take this torment any longer.

Chapter Sixteen

My night is awful.

I think it was the worst night's sleep I have ever had to endure in my twenty-nine years. My eyes feel like a ten-pound weight is hanging from them, and my head feels like thousands of mini golf balls are pinging around, trying to get a birdie.

I spent the entire night tossing and turning, with too many thoughts rushing through my mind. First, I let my mind stress about my flat and the situation I'm currently in, and then I can't help but focus on the promotion. Then, my thoughts wander to Lucas and Delilah and to the land of loneliness, where I'm lying in a field of wheat, surrounded by not one single soul.

I finished the night of the internal monologue with a splendid reel of *"Will my life ever get better?"* before I drifted into a plagued sleep of worries and torment.

I barely had three hours of sleep before my phone started going off.

It's an email from Dylan, my boss. He wants me to sit in on

a meeting this morning, which means I have approximately thirty minutes to get up, get dressed, and dash to work.

I can't wait to go to a meeting because I don't want to spend today with Lucas, talking about *Delilah*. It may feel a little … intimate. My flat is still the Pacific Ocean, and spending the day with my boss is far more appealing than with Lucas and my confusing emotions.

I quickly fire an email, RSVPing, and I start to get ready.

I need a shower, but I don't know how I feel about using *his* shower. For some reason, the very thought seems way too intimate.

Instead, I decide to leave it this morning, and figure something out later.

I open the bedroom door, extremely quietly, not wanting to wake Lucas up who slept on the sofa last night. I creep to grab my jacket and bag and quietly head out the door.

I attempt to close the door quietly, grimacing as it squeaks ever so slightly. I seriously do not want him to wake up and have to attempt small talk. Especially after last night's revelations.

As the door clicks shut, I inhale and exhale a sigh of relief, and I quickly turn, bumping into someone in the process. My bag falls to the floor, and half of its contents spill out onto the floor.

"Shit, I'm sorry—" I gasp, but stop in my tracks as I realise, I just bumped into Lucas.

"Oh, it's you," I say, bending to pick up my stuff.

"Yes, it's me. Next to my flat," he says, humour swirling around in his beautiful eyes. "It's a shock you'd see me here," he says, chuckling to himself.

He bends to help me pick up the things from my bag. I

quietly thank him, not sure what else I can say. Usually I can feign banter, but with Lucas, I find this incredibly difficult. I'm starting to become tongue tied around him. *What's that about?*

"What are you up to today?" he asks, his eyes meeting mine.

"I have a meeting with my boss about a promotion," I explain, standing up from the floor and brushing off my knees.

Lucas looks at me, his eyes widening slightly. "A promotion? That's incredible!" he exclaims, his smile beaming for me.

"Thank you. I'm working really hard to try and earn this promotion, so working on a Saturday will become my reality." I laugh.

He opens his mouth as if about to speak, but as he truly lays his eyes on me, he seems to lose his train of thought. Finally, he says, "You look … awful."

Caught off guard, a small gasp escapes my lips. "Ah, so I'm not the kind of beautiful girl you'd expect to be leaving your flat at this ungodly hour?" I fire back, sarcasm dripping from my words as I clutch my bag in front of me like a shield, feeling as though my vulnerability is lying bare in front of him. I can't think of anything worse than being vulnerable.

He looks flustered, shaking his head as if to reboot his thought process. "No, no, I mean—you look beautiful," he stammers, his fingers awkwardly scratching his chin as if searching for the right words. "It's just that you also look tired. Did you sleep alright? If the bed isn't comfortable or something, maybe we could … I don't know, brainstorm a new setup?"

His awkwardness almost mirrors mine, but my thoughts are still snagged on how he called me beautiful. It creates a warm, distracting buzz in my mind.

"Ah, I'm okay," I finally say, letting out a hesitant laugh. "I just have a lot on my plate." As I say this, the weight of all my restless thoughts—about the wedding, the promotion, and my flat troubles—swells up again, rushing back into the forefront of my mind.

"Let me help you. I'm happy to be your date for the wedding. Let me take this off your shoulders at least," he offers again.

This time I consider it, needing one less thing to worry about. After all, the wedding is next weekend, and I'm no closer to finding *'The One'*

Or that's what I'm telling myself. It has *nothing* to do with Lucas and Delilah…

"Okay, but promise me you will do exactly as I say," I say, looking intently in his eyes.

"That was a lot easier than I expected, and of course. I can handle it," he promises.

Chapter Seventeen

I walk into the conference room with a sense of anticipation swirling in my gut. The PowerPoint presentation is already set up on the big screen at the end of the room, and I see Rachel is already seated, laptop open and ready. Dylan strides in right behind me, with a coffee in his hand and a smirk on his face. He blows on the coffee in his hands through the tiny hole you drink from. I make a face, shocked that this man is going to decide my future.

This meeting is crucial, it's all about showing Dylan that Rachel and I are increasing our numbers, which proves that I deserve the promotion over everyone else at the office.

I shoot Rachel my most encouraging smiles, and sit beside her, gently squeezing her hand. She squeezes mine back, both of us feeling the weight of this meeting.

"Shall we get started?" Dylan asks, diving right into the slides. My stomach drops to the floor, and my veins feel as though they're ready to burst from the pressure. I sit still, though. My face remains emotionless as I tackle my nerves head on.

We dissect pre-order sales, go over the success rates of our campaigns, and discuss market penetrations.

Dylan points his laser pointer at the PowerPoint like a Jedi Knight wielding a lightsaber. The room feels like the set of *Shark Tank*, only here the sharks are us, trying to get a promotion instead of an investment.

Just as Dylan goes over future expectations of Rachel and I, my phone buzzes and flashes on the table. I glance down to see Maddy's text:

Hey Rosie, we're having the rehearsal this weekend. I think it'll be great for you to come (with Lucas! Just take him up on his offer!)

Rachel leans in closer to me than a detective during a criminals interrogation, subtly reading the message as Dylan continues to passionately discuss the money we could make with this book like a preacher.

"Spill the beans, have you asked Lucas or not?" Rachel's whisper comes with the excitement of a kid who has just been told they can go to McDonalds.

"As a matter of fact, yes, Sherlock, I have," I whisper back, rolling my eyes for added flair.

Rachel lets out a tiny squeal, but it's enough to make Dylan swivel his head towards us like a human periscope.

"Is there an issue?" Dylan asks, raising one eyebrow so high it almost joins his receding hairline.

I shake my head, mentally cursing Rachel. There's a promotion hanging in the balance here! "No, no problem at all," I stammer, "We're just excited about this release, and listening to you talk about the potential ROI and how well this book is being received, is inspirational," I lie. Rachel is nodding her head erratically beside me.

Dylan squints, his scepticism momentarily showing before melting into satisfaction. "I have to say, I totally agree. You women have done an amazing job, and you should both be proud of yourselves! Keep up the good work, and you could be looking at the promotion in a few weeks time," he states, his commendation enveloping me as well.

Dylan checks the time. "Okay, I won't keep you ladies any longer on a Saturday, so let's wrap this up," he says.

Rachel slips on her sunglasses as we step out of the office, into the bright afternoon sunlight. "Alright, spill. When did you ask Lucas? How did it go? Details, Rosie, details!"

I let out a sigh, adjusting the strap of my purse on my shoulder. "It happened this morning outside his flat, and *he* asked *me.*"

Rachel gasps, her eyes glowing with excitement. "He asked you? How romantic! What did you say?" she asks, fully invested in this.

"I obviously said, yes!" I say, laughing.

"And?" she prompts.

"And that's it. I just accepted."

She frowns as she finally looks at me. "What's wrong?"

I hesitate, my words fumbling as I try to articulate my thoughts. "I just ... What if my family finds out it's all an act? I'll never live it down, Rachel. My cousins already think I'm desperate enough to fake it."

Rachel gives me a knowing look. "First of all, your family loves you. Secondly, No one's going to suspect a thing."

"Yeah, but lying to my family? What if we slip up?"

Rachel stops walking and looks at me, putting her hands on my shoulders. "Rosie, listen to me. You're not doing anything wrong. You're just trying to get through a family event without unnecessary stress. And let's face it, every family has its quirks. Yours just happens to be overly interested in your love life."

I chuckle, nodding reluctantly. "Yeah, you're right."

She starts walking again, pulling me along. "Besides, it's not like you're planning a long-term deception here—it's just for the wedding. You can brief Lucas on a few key facts so you're on the same page."

"Like a fake how-we-met story?"

"Exactly. And as far as anniversaries and mutual friends go, just say you're keeping things low-key and private."

Still feeling a little unsettled, but a lot better, I gently squeeze her arm in thanks. "Alright, alright. Maybe you're right. I'm just overthinking things."

Rachel links her arm through mine. "You usually do. But that's why you have me, to pull you back from the edge of your own imagination."

We reach Rachel's car, and as she unlocks it, I suddenly feel grateful. Not just for Lucas's willingness to be my wedding date, but for Rachel's friendship and her never-ending ability to make me see reason.

"Thanks, Rachel."

She winks at me. "Anytime. Now, let's get going. You have a 'how-we-met' story to fabricate, and maybe even a fake anniversary to celebrate. How does January 23rd sound?"

I laugh. "Perfect. January 23rd it is."

****

As I approach, not my own flat, but Lucas's, the air feels dense with tension. The cosy little space I've called home since I left university has been more than a sanctuary—it's been a retreat, a small island in the world that belonged solely to me. I was never the quintessential twenty-something, sipping cocktails in crowded bars or swiping right on dating apps. No, I found solace in my own company, with my career as my sole focus.

The thought which used to comfort me now pinches—could my relentless focus on my career and solitude mean that I've let "the one" slip through my fingers? Shivers crawl up my spine at the prospect.

With a resolute shake of my head, as though I could physically dispel the awful, scary and disquieting thoughts, I reach for the spare key Lucas had handed me. The metal feels cool against my palm as I slip it into the lock and enter his flat, the contrast to my flat is just as startling as the first time I came here.

"Lucas?" I call into the emptiness.

There is no response. I set my purse gently on the table and drape my jacket on the coat rack with a sigh.

I take out my phone—recently updated with Lucas's personal number post that ridiculous flood incident—and hit "Dial." He answers almost immediately.

"Already miss me?" he teases, and I can practically hear his smirk over the line.

"Only you could answer a phone that fast," I retort, steadying myself for the question that's making my heart flutter anxiously. After all, Lucas meeting my family is almost parallel to jumping into a tornado. "Where are you?" I ask, trying to delay the question.

"I'm just out running a few errands. What's up?" he asks. I can still hear a slight smile in his voice, which calms me slightly.

Taking a steadying breath, I fumble, "Maddy texted me. Her rehearsal is this weekend..." and I let my words trail off, hesitating to articulate the actual question. Our relationship—or rather our "arrangement"—still feels so odd.

I can hear Lucas breathing on the other end of the line, waiting.

"So?" I press, my voice tinged with hopeful desperation, praying he read between the lines.

Lucas chuckles. "You haven't actually posed a question for me to answer," he points out.

I roll my eyes. "Would you like to come with me?" I exhale, my words rushing out.

There's a loaded pause. "My schedule's awfully busy," he teases.

I roll my eyes again. "I'll throw in a pizza," I say, laughing at my own attempt at a joke.

He groans. "I think I'll pass on the pizza," he says. I laugh harder, remembering my silly prank.

His laughter reverberates through the phone. "Of course I'll go. We can discuss the details later when you're back." For some reason, when he said "when you're back" my heart skipped a beat.

I ignore it and carry on.

"Thank you, Lucas," I breathe, feeling a weight lift off my shoulders.

"Before you hang up, how does take out sound? I'm ordering Chinese tonight," he suggests, his voice easy and light.

The mention of food sends a wave of hunger through me, and I'm suddenly aware of my incredibly empty stomach. "Sounds perfect."

"Look at us, fake dating and playing house," he quips, a touch of irony in his tone.

"I'm hanging up now." I laugh. As I toss my phone back into

my bag, I catch my reflection in the hall mirror—my expression softened, cheeks flushed and a small smile pulling on my lips. What on earth is happening to me?

****

The door opens, making me jump on the sofa, my book almost falling out of my hands. It's almost five in the evening and Lucas is standing in the doorway, holding a bag of take out food.

I raise my eyebrow at him, and Lucas looks down, smirking.

"I have Chinese. It's getting cold. Come on, I'm starving!" he insists, walking towards the kitchen. I laugh and follow behind him, the delicious smell of Chinese hitting my nostrils and my mouth starts to water.

"That smells incredible, but I didn't tell you my order," I challenge, hoping he didn't get anything with mushrooms. I seriously cannot stand that fungus.

He starts taking some boxes out of the bag. "This is chicken Chow Mein, and I guessed you like that since everyone loves Chow Mein," he says pointing towards one of the boxes. "This is spicy rice. I remember that you like spicy food and that you're not a woman who thinks toothpaste is spicy," he says, blowing out a relieved sigh as he continues to point out more boxes and naming the contents. He has chips, curry samosas and spring rolls, chicken balls and most of the sauces. I'm surprised, because everything he's got, I really enjoy. Nothing has mushrooms, thankfully.

"Is that to your liking?" he asks, gesturing towards the food.

"You've done well. You must do this all the time," I joke. I walk around him and grab some plates, cutlery, and the kitchen roll and place them on the kitchen table. Lucas is still standing

152

there, looking at me with an expression I can't quite place.

"Come on, I'm starving!" I say, putting the plates on the table.

He places the various boxes in the middle of the table without saying anything else.

I start filling my plate up with food, and it feels like ages since I last had a takeaway with someone.

We sit in silence eating our food, and again, I feel like this is natural. I look up at Lucas, watching as he does a little hand dance every time he eats something delicious. I watch as he opens his mouth, savouring the taste of every bite and I find myself feeling hotter. He takes a swig of his beer and I watch as his throat bobs with every swallow and how his jawline becomes sharp and intimidating. I watch as he delicately picks up the food, holding it with purpose.

"How's the food?" he asks.

I'm instantly drawn out of my daydream, humiliated that I was caught gawking at him.

"It's good," I answer, feeling the blush creep up my cheeks. Lucas doesn't seem bothered or uncomfortable in any way, and he just goes back to eating his food. Maybe he didn't see me gawking at him. Either way, I need to stop all of this. Especially if we're about to work together.

"Thank you for agreeing to be my date for the wedding," I say, scratching at my arms.

He looks up, his eyes on mine. "No need to thank me," he says, his eyes burning a hole into my soul. I look down, not entirely sure why I'm having a hard time looking at him.

"Well, I just wanted to say I appreciate it," I say, truly meaning it.

We fall into a comfortable silence, eating our food and

pretending like we don't feel awkward around each other. As we finish our food, Lucas pours two glasses of wine, deciding to retire his beers.

He looks down before he grabs our plates and places them on the side, near the sink. He turns on the hot water tap, filling the bowl with warm, soapy water. Even though I can hear the water trickling into the sink, the room feels quiet.

"Can I help at all?" I ask, finishing off my wine.

"It's all good. You're the guest," he answers, giving me a sweet smile. "Would you like more wine?"

I nod, handing him my glass. "Why not?" I ask. Lucas smirks before he pours me another glass of red. "So, how did you get into sports writing?" I ask, wanting to change the atmosphere around here. I lean against the counter, staring at the bowl filling up.

"Long story short, I like sports, but I was never a player. I always watched, and after I went travelling after university, I bumped into someone who was a sports journalist and I found it fascinating, so I kind of fell into this career. It wasn't planned."

"So, you travel?" I ask.

"Yeah, from time to time. I moved away for university and once I graduated, I went travelling. I moved back here once I landed a sports column," he answers, placing the cutlery in the warm soapy water.

"Do you enjoy being back? Or do you prefer to travel?" I ask, feeling a pang of jealousy that he's left this country. I haven't even been on a plane as I've been too focused on my career to even entertain the idea of travelling.

"I will always love travelling. I'm hoping to travel in a few years. I have an idea for a series, sort of like a travel diary," he explains, his passion lighting up his face like a volcano getting ready to erupt.

I look down at his arm. "Is that why you got that tattoo?" I ask. Since the first day I met him, I've noticed his tattoo, but I never knew what it meant.

He lifts his arm, his hands dripping with water into the sink and dries his hands with a towel. "I actually had this tattoo done when I was in Italy," he says. When he's looking at the tattoo, his eyes gloss over. As I watch him, it feels like we're no longer in the kitchen, we're standing on the Ponte Di Rialto bridge.

"What were you doing there?" I ask, wanting to know more about the man I've lived next door to for many years. I'm slightly embarrassed I'm only now getting to know him.

His lips pull in a small smile. "I went there for work after university. I had no idea what I wanted to do, but I also knew I needed to see the world. I networked and I worked in hospitality, barely making enough to buy a coffee"—he laughed at this notion as if it were silly to him now—"and now I make enough money to buy a car. It's all trivial and materialistic, but I look at this tattoo and I realise how far I've travelled. I remember how hard I've worked for the recognition I now receive, and it keeps me…" he pauses, thinking of a way to describe how he's feeling.

"Grounded," I finish for him. He looks at me, nodding. In this moment, we share our feelings and I've never felt so connected to someone before.

As we continue to drink wine, standing in the kitchen, talking, the more I feel comfortable. Lucas uncorks the second bottle of wine with a slight struggle, finally managing to pry it free. "Aha! Take that, cork!"

I chuckle as I watch him pour more deep-red liquid into our glasses. "You make it seem like an epic battle between man and cork."

"It is," Lucas grins, handing me a glass. "A tale as old as time."

We both take a sip, the rich flavours going straight to my head as our laughter mingles in the air. As the night goes on, the closer we become. Before long, I'm sitting on the counter top with Lucas standing beside me, his arm lightly leaning on my leg as we talk.

"So, what's your favourite type of music?" I ask, my voice slurring a little more than I'd like, the wine making it easier to ask him about his life.

"I love rock, alternative, even some of the old jazz standards. How about you?"

"I'm all over the place. Indie, pop, rock. Although, I've recently taken a liking to folk music."

"Folk music, eh? You're just full of surprises."

I blush a little. "I like to keep people on their toes."

Our eyes are starting to meet more frequently, our gazes lingering just a tad longer than they would've earlier in the evening.

My eyes drop to his lips. I know he knows I'm looking at his lips, but I can't seem to drag my eyes away. He slowly licks his bottom lip and turns his body towards me.

I don't say a word as I silently beg him to make the decision and to finally close the gap between us.

My eyes meet his eyes again, and I'm almost knocked back by the way he's looking at me. Right now, I'm a deer trapped in a lion's enclosure. I'm his prey, and it doesn't scare me. There's something animalistic in the way he's looking at me.

Realising the drink may be causing me to think out of

character, I look away, clearing my throat. "I better get some sleep," I announce.

Lucas clears his throat, and scratches his chin as he nods in agreement. "I agree. Here let me help you," he says before he helps me down, off the counter. As we're both a bit drunk, we fumble a little before he manages to securely place his arms around my waist. The touch is electrifying, sending tiny shivers down my spine. I notice the way his arms feel solid and warm as he holds onto me. Lucas gazes at me with a look that seems to penetrate my very soul, his eyes dark and intense.

There's a brief, charged moment where the air between us thickens, where time seems to pause and the world around us fades away. Our eyes lock, and for a split second, we want the same thing. Then, as if snapping back from a dream, Lucas gently lowers me down to the floor, his arms retracting but not before giving me a reassuring squeeze. I find myself standing on my own two feet, yet feeling a slight loss at the absence of his touch.

We both clear our throats almost simultaneously, as if acknowledging the tension without daring to voice it.

"Goodnight," Lucas says softly, his voice laced with a hint of regret, as if there are a thousand more words he wishes to say.

"Goodnight," I echo, taking a step back to put some physical distance between us, as if that could also increase the emotional distance.

Chapter Eighteen

My eyes flutter open, my head heavy from the drinks Lucas and I shared the night before. As I stir, trying to make sense of my surroundings, my heart skips a beat when I realise I'm no longer in bed, and I'm not alone.

Somehow I end up back out in the living room, lying on the sofa, and beside me, wrapped in a warm, inviting embrace, is Lucas. His arm is draped over me, pulling me in close. For a moment, I simply lay there, my heart racing as I absorb the reality of the situation. How the hell did I end up here?

I can feel the rise and fall of Lucas's chest against my chest, the steady rhythm of his breathing. I look up, to see he's sleeping. My eyes trace the contours of his face as he sleeps. His features are relaxed, his lips curved in a subtle, contented smile.

Lucas stirs, his eyes slowly fluttering open. My heart starts to pound in my chest as I worry about what he's going to say. How did I end up here?

Without saying a word, Lucas pulls me closer to him, and starts to leave sleepy kisses on my shoulder. He doesn't question me on what I'm doing and why I'm here.

I push myself closer to him, as if I'm possessed by something primal. His eyes become darker the closer my body becomes.

I'm not sure what I'm about to do, but my mind is no longer in control.

"Rosie," he says, his voice strained as I look up at his face, enjoying the way he's reacting to me. I didn't realise teasing a man can feel this powerful and glorious, but here I am, enjoying every moment.

"Lucas," I whisper back, biting my lip, waiting for him to make the first move. He lets out a low groan as he watches my teeth gently graze my lip. My heart can't wait a second longer, and he finally starts to lean in. His hands snake around my waist, pulling me into his hard, hot body as I wrap my leg around his waist, eager to feel his lips on mine.

His lips crash on mine and I groan as it feels as good as I'd always imagined, if not better. I grab hold of him, needing to be closer than we are right now. His hands slip under my shirt, caressing my skin.

Feeling brave, and not wanting to waste this moment, I push him on his back and straddle him with my legs before I kiss him again.

Lucas pulls back slightly. "Didn't want to do this in the bed?" he asks, his voice ragged and harsh.

"I don't know why I'm here," I admit, my breathing as harsh as his.

He pulls me towards him and nibbles my neck, trailing down to my collarbone. "You wanted this," he whispers.

With a gasp, I startle awake into the darkness of Lucas's

bedroom, exactly where I was last night. The sheets are wet from my sweat as they stick to my body, and the room is cloaked in silence. All I can hear is my harsh breathing as I try to make sense of what just happened. My hands are caressing my body in a way they haven't done in a long time as I remember the dream I just had.

Removing my hand and bolting upright, I lean forward, my senses on high alert. I strain my ears, searching for any sign of life beyond the door. There's a subtle rustle, a faint creak of the floorboards. Glancing at the clock, it reads 3:49 A.M. A shiver of worry runs down my spine. Is Lucas awake? Did I disturb his sleep with potential moaning or God forbid, calling his name?

I just had a sex dream about Lucas, and he's right outside the door.

Absolutely amazing. This is just what I need!

***

After a terrible night of tossing and turning, and wondering if Lucas heard me, I finally have the confidence to go into the kitchen and grab something to eat. I go to creep past the sofa, trying not to wake Lucas.

Before I realise that Lucas isn't there, a deep, gravelly voice says, "Hey."

I jump back, pressing my palm to my chest as my heart beats into overdrive. "Bloody hell—" I say as my eyes meet Lucas's. He's leaning on the kitchen counter, holding a bowl of cereal in his strong hands. The same strong hands that had held me last night—

No. It wasn't his hands. It was a dream.

As soon as I remember my dream, I start to blush.

Lucas looks like a statue as he eats his cereal, watching me from over the bowl. His jogging bottoms hang low on his hips, and I can't stop myself from appreciating the "V" that points to his prize. A prize I almost dreamt of. I dart my eyes away as quickly as I can.

I clear my throat. "Morning."

"Morning."

"How did you sleep?"

He nods, his eyes watching me carefully. "Like a rock. You?"

I scratch my arms, trying to look at anything else but Lucas. "Yeah, it was okay. It was quite warm," I say, remembering the way the sheets stuck to my skin.

"Very hot," he says, taking another bite of cereal off his spoon. I'm convinced he heard me.

Shit.

"Are you up to much today?" I ask, trying to distract him.

He places the bowl on the counter before he looks back at me, his eyes revealing that he knows something. "Actually, I was going to ask if you were busy today? I wanted to go out and buy an outfit for the rehearsal and I may need your help," he says, his eyes pleading with me.

I can't help but grin at Lucas's request, the embarrassment of last night didn't disappear, but it was forgotten for a moment.

"Oh, you know, I just might have some free time today," I reply, pretending to ponder the idea. "I suppose I could help you pick out an outfit."

Lucas's face lights up, and he lets out an exaggerated sigh of relief. "I can't trust my fashion sense alone, especially to be questioned by your family"

I chuckle at his theatrics. "Well, you're in luck. My fashion expertise is at your service."

***

We stroll down the bustling shopping street, on a mission to find the perfect outfit for Lucas. Walking beside him feels strange, but it's nice.

I glance at Lucas, a playful smile on my lips. "So, Lucas, what's your fashion style? Are you more of a classic suit guy, or do you lean toward something more trendy?"

Lucas chuckles, adjusting his sunglasses. "I'm versatile. I can rock a classic suit or a more casual look, depending on the occasion. But for this party, I'm thinking of something classic yet stylish, so I don't steal too much thunder from the happy couple."

I nod, appreciating his consideration. "Great—classic with a twist it is. Let's start with this store over here."

We enter a men's boutique, and Lucas begins to browse through the racks of suits while I peruse the ties. Lucas holds up a charcoal-grey suit jacket, raising an eyebrow in question.

I tilt my head, assessing the choice. "Hmm, that's nice, but how about we add a pop of colour with the tie? Something that compliments my dress?"

Lucas grins, clearly enjoying the collaborative shopping experience. "I like that idea. What colour are you wearing?"

Feeling confident, I lean in even closer, my lips almost grazing his ear. "It's a deep emerald green," I whisper, my breath warm against his skin, "very elegant, and very figure-hugging."

Lucas swallows hard, his eyes locked on mine. "Wow," he manages to say, his voice slightly shaky. "Okay, green it is."

We spend the next hour exploring the store, pulling out various ties and shirts, mixing and matching until we find the perfect combination. Every now and then, our fingers brush against each other, sending electric sparks down my spine.

As we head to the dressing rooms, Lucas can't resist a teasing remark. "I have to say, Rosie, I never thought I'd enjoy shopping for clothes this much. You've got a great eye."

I laugh, a twinkle in my eye. "Who knew fake dating could be so much fun, right?"

Inside the dressing rooms, Lucas tries on the selected outfit. As Lucas steps out of the dressing room, a rush of admiration floods over me. His transformation from the casually dressed guy I'd met earlier to this refined and impeccably dressed man is striking. My heart skips a beat, and I find it hard to tear my gaze away.

His charcoal-grey suit jacket fits him perfectly, emphasising his broad shoulders and lean frame. The dark fabric complements his tousled chestnut hair and chiselled jawline. The emerald green tie, expertly chosen to match my dress, adds a dash of vibrant colour to his attire, drawing attention to his strong, masculine neck.

My eyes travel down to the crisp white shirt, tailored to perfection, highlighting his toned physique without being overly tight. The suit trousers, dark and well-fitted, accentuate his long legs—the overall look exuding sophistication.

Lucas stands confidently, his hands casually resting in his pockets, and I can't help but think how incredibly handsome he looks. It's not just the clothes—it's the way he carries himself, the self-assuredness in his posture, and the twinkle of mischief in his eyes.

"Wow, Lucas"—I breathe, my gaze raking over him appreciatively—"you …Wow."

Lucas grins, doing a little spin. "Well, thank you, Rosie. It's all thanks to your impeccable taste."

I clear my throat and regain my composure. "Okay, we're

almost done. Now we just need to find you some shoes and accessories."

Lucas nods in agreement, heading back into the dressing room to change. As we venture to the shoe section, I can't help but reflect on the unexpected fun we're having.

Lucas tries on several pairs of shoes, from classic black to a stylish pair of brown leather loafers. I give my input, considering not only style, but also comfort, as we have a long night of pretending ahead.

Finally, we settle on a pair of dark brown shoes that complement Lucas's outfit perfectly. I hand him a matching belt, a pair of cufflinks, and a watch to complete the ensemble.

Lucas checks himself out in a full-length mirror, a satisfied grin on his face. "I have to admit, Rosie, I feel quite dapper in this outfit. You really know your stuff."

I wink. "It's all about the details. Now, let's get you to the cashier so we can make this outfit officially yours."

At the checkout counter, Lucas and I pay for the suit, tie, shoes, and accessories, and Lucas can't help but feel grateful for my guidance and company.

As we walk out of the store, bags in hand, the sun has started to dip below the horizon, casting a warm, golden light over the city. Lucas turns to me, a genuine smile on his face.

"This was fun. I'm looking forward to rocking this outfit at the rehearsal."

I smile back at him, actually happier about this fake dating thing than I was before. "It's going to be a memorable night, that's for sure."

****

Once we're back at the flat, I jump in the shower, ready to

settle down for the night. I can't help but think about today and how much fun I had with Lucas. There's something about him that intrigues me, and I intend to find out what that is.

After the refreshing shower, I wrap the towel around myself. As I do, I can hear a distant knock.

"Lucas, is someone at the door?" I shout, patting my hair dry with another towel.

There's no answer.

I head out of the bathroom just as Lucas opens the door, and nothing could have prepared me for who is standing outside.

Her eyes dart to mine, before looking down at my lack of clothes. Shit.

"Firstly, everyone is right—you are very handsome! And secondly, I didn't know you two were living together! That's wonderful!" my mother says, clapping her hands in delight. She looks back at me, her smile widening slightly. "Did I interrupt your romantic evening? I am sorry, but we have very important matters to attend to. I was knocking on your door, Rosie, then I saw the note saying you're staying here and here you are," she says, throwing me a wink like she's proud I'm finally living with a man.

I rush to grab my shirt as I quickly pull the wet fabric over my head, covering myself. This woman really has the worst timing in the entire world.

Lucas closes the door slightly in a way to cover me from her eyes.

My mother gently pushes the door open, stepping into the room. "I know, I've been incredibly busy! But, I thought I'd pop by and see Rosie, in the hopes of meeting you as well … And here you are. Double whammy!"

Lucas looks at me, his eyes widening waiting for me to

introduce him to my mother, confusion replacing the lust he once held on to his face.

"Lucas, this is my mother, Taylor. Mother, this is Lucas, my … boyfriend," I say. As if Lucas just realises that he's still half-naked, his eyes widen as realisation sets in. He quickly grabs his shirt, pulling it over his head as he sheepishly shakes my mother's hand.

"It's nice to meet you," he says.

Before we can say anything else, my mother drops an overnight bag on the floor next to the stairs.

"Uh? What's that?" I ask, already knowing where this is going.

My mother looks around the room as if there's nothing there. "What?"

I point to the bag. "That. What's that?" I ask again.

"Oh! I was hoping I could stay with you for a few days until the wedding," she says, pressing her hands together in prayer.

"Lucas, can you just help me bring in some coffees and teas?" I ask, widening my eyes as if to say he has no choice in the matter. I quickly rush into the kitchen as my mother watches us with a huge smile on her face.

Once we're in the kitchen, I quietly shut the door to prevent her from hearing us. Once I'm happy she can't hear, I turn to Lucas, unable to hide the embarrassment on my face.

"What are we going to do?" he asks,

I sigh, leaning on the counter. "Well, she can't stay at mine because it's still flooded. She'll have to stay here…"

"How will that work? We aren't actually together!" Lucas whispers.

"I don't know! Maybe we have to come clean?" I say, panic paralysing my voice.

"No, we're in it until the end. We'll just have to fake it when she's here," he suggests. Once he says that, we both realise how difficult that's going to be.

"So, you suggest we fake it? How will that work?" I ask, holding the bridge of my nose. I brace myself for his response.

He leans against the counter, casually, and a defeated sigh leaves his lips as if he can't think of another solution. "We will have to sleep together, hold hands, cuddle, and even kiss when she's around. It's the only thing I can think of," Lucas says, like his mind is already made up, and I'm just going along with this plan.

I can't imagine this not being complicated, especially after the kiss we just shared.

"You can't be serious." I shoot him a look. "You don't think this will work? What if it makes things … complicated?" I ask, voicing my concerns and blushing at the thought of our skin pressed together moments before, being a lot more frequent.

"It won't," he says. I blink and start laughing at the thought.

"Have you got any other options? A *better* option?" I ask, hoping he does. He makes a face. My shoulders fall in defeat. "Do you even have any other options?"

"Well, maybe we can suggest she sleeps with me and you stay on the sofa? That way, we have an excuse." My cheeks heat with a fierce blush.

"Okay, we can try that."

"Okay."

"Then it's settled," he says, gently tapping the counter with resolve.

I shake my head. "Thank you for doing this. I just can't believe you're going to help this," I say, my voice soft as I try to portray my appreciation to him.

He sighs, taking a small step towards me. "I don't know why you don't think I'll help you. I've been here all along," he says, and I want to sink into his words, but the memory of what he said outside my door all those years ago jumps straight to the front of my mind.

"Because I didn't think you liked me," I whisper, avoiding all eye contact with him. I'm finally finding the courage to admit this to him, and I don't want to see his reaction.

"Why would you think that?" he asks, his voice completely unaware of what he said.

"When you first moved in, I overheard you telling your friends you'd never be seen with someone like me. You said more than that, but I don't really want to go into it," I say, crossing my arms over my chest, trying to seem nonchalant about it.

Lucas is quiet for a moment, and I don't look up. I don't think I can, in case his face portrays everything I'm terrified of.

He steps a little closer, and my heart begins to race. His hand reaches out and his fingers gently touch my chin, forcing me to look at him. His eyes are warm and kind as he looks at me. "I said that because I really liked you. I didn't want my friends, who aren't my friends any more because they're cocks, knowing I liked you. They would've used it against me or tried to get you for themselves. I said it because I didn't want to ruin our relationship and I know it sounds like I'm making it up, but I swear it's the truth."

"Okay," I say, deciding to let this whole thing go. I have his explanation now, and I believe him. I can't hold a grudge and ask him to help me out with something so humiliating.

"Then let's do it," I say. He nods again, and this time, his stare is solidified, and determination is evident on his face. We both stare at each other in silence as my lips tingle from the memory of his lips on mine. The air is thick with tension as his eyes flash with a desire I'd only seen in his eyes a few moments before.

I clear my throat, needing to calm myself down. "We need to discuss a lot of details to pull this off." I say. "More than just the basics we discussed the other day. This is my mother, and she can see through my bullshit."

Lucas nods, taking a step back. "We can figure this out."

Before we can say anything else, there's a light knock on the kitchen door. Just on time, as always. She never fails to disappoint.

Lucas and I both stand up straight, and I look at him in panic, worried we won't be able to pull this off. If we can't, then I'll one thousand percent be the laughingstock of the family.

My mother peeks her head through the small crack in the door.

"I hope you're not having sex in there," she says, chuckling to herself like she just said the world's funniest joke.

I pull a face. "Of course not!" I huff.

As she comes in through the door, satisfied she hasn't walked in on something, Lucas grabs my hand in one swift swoop. My heart goes into my stomach as the warmth from his hand engulfs mine, providing me with the comfort I've craved since we kissed. I sink into his touch, all worry from my mind ceasing to exist in this current moment.

"Rosie has told me so much about you" he says, turning on his charm without a second thought.

She swoons. I would roll my eyes if I wasn't melting under his touch.

"Like what? You can't say that and leave me hanging!" She laughs, waiting for his compliments.

Lucas cleared his throat, trying to come up with something, anything, that he could say to my mother. He squeezes my hand, looking for some help.

"Well," I begin, a warm smile on my face, "I told him about the time we spent all day building a tree house, only for it to crumble with some wind and rain. I told him how you went out the very next day and rebuilt it before I came back from school."

My mother's eyes sparkled with nostalgia. "Gosh, that was a long time ago. You loved that tree house, I could barely pull you away from it."

She comes over to me and gives me a hug before pulling back and holding my face in her hands, gently. She looks me in the eyes, and she gives me the speech I know she's been waiting for. "I'm so happy you're happy. You've truly hit the jackpot, and I've never been prouder." She's beaming. On the outside, I'm so happy she's said that, but inside, it's a startling reminder that this isn't my life.

I pull away from my mother, and Lucas pulls me into his strong, muscled arms. My lip pulls in a small smile.

She clasps her hands together, watching us in awe. Part of me wants this, but another part of me knows it isn't real.

"What are you doing here?" I ask.

My mother looks hurt for a second before she smiles. "I just thought I'd spend some time with you," she says, but I can see through it. I love my mother, but I know she's checking up on Lucas and to see if he's good enough for me. Since my father cheated on her, she's been terrified that I'll share the same fate. "Plus, the rehearsal is soon, and since I moved, I didn't want to spend the day travelling. I thought I'd kill two birds with one stone. It's not a crime!" she says, chuckling to herself.

"We better get some sleep. Tracey, you and Rosie can sleep in my bed, and I'll take the sofa," Lucas offers.

My mother shakes her head, tutting. "No, no, no. My daughter's boyfriend is not sleeping on his own sofa. You can sleep with your girlfriend in your own bed. I'll take the sofa as I've just burst in! I'm not old-fashioned," she says, winking at us.

Oh, God.

"We really don't mind," I say, slightly panicking.

"Hush. I've already decided."

I look at Lucas, trying to see if he has a solution. By the look on his clueless face, I'd say she's cornered us.

He shrugs at me, and then smiles at my mother, sweetly. "If you're sure. But I'm happy to take the sofa," he offers again. She shakes her head, and I know she won't relent. She's stubborn, which means we'll be sleeping together tonight.

Wonderful.

Chapter Nineteen

I head into Lucas's room, unable to relax as the thought of us sharing the same bed torments me. I've never done anything like this before.

As I look down at the bed I've already slept in, I can't help but imagine how close we're going to be. How close our heads will be and how warm our bodies will feel sleeping next to each other. What if he turns over in his sleep and he hugs into me?

No, I need to remember that I'm an adult, and I can handle sleeping next to another man for one night.

Lucas comes in behind me, closing the bedroom door. We are completely alone and enclosed in this small room, his presence is alarmingly obvious. I shoot him a small smile, and I can't help but notice the way his eyes burn as he looks at me, standing there in only a towel. Even in the dark room, I can see and feel the tension wrapping around us.

"Take a picture, it'll last longer," I joke, my voice is husky as I fight the urge to jump on him and take what I've wanted since his lips claimed mine.

Lucas shifts uncomfortably on his feet beside the door, not saying a word. My heart beats in my chest as we continue to stare, neither one of us making a sound. With each lingering moment that passed, the more my heavy breathing filled the room as my chest rose and fell. Lucas's eyes flicker to my chest, tensing his jaw as he visibly restrains himself. I've never had a man look at me the way Lucas has looked at me in the last three hours, and I wanted more of it.

He takes a step back, scratching his chin. "I'll look away while you get changed," he says before he heads to the bed and sits facing the opposite wall, so his back is to me. I open the drawer Lucas gave me to put some of my clothes in and pulled out a baggy t-shirt and shorts. The more I wear, the better, I think to myself.

Once I'm changed, I walk towards the bed, peel back the covers and jump in.

"I'm ready," I say, feeling anxious again as Lucas turns around and lays down beside me, on top of the comforter. We lay there in silence for a few moments whilst staring at the ceiling.

"Your mother is very…" Lucas tries to say, but struggles to find the words to describe

her.

"Totally opposite to me?" I suggest rubbing my temples, trying to distract myself.

He chuckles. "I see a lot of similarities in you both," he says.

"How are we even remotely similar? Besides sharing some DNA," I ask, not entirely focusing on this conversation. I should have been more offended than I am, but I have more important things to worry about.

"I think DNA is a lot more important than you make it

sound," he says, chuckling as he adjusts on the bed, sinking further into the mattress. "But you're both passionate and won't take no for an answer. I think it's a good thing," he says, his voice becoming sleepier.

I frown. "How does forcing herself into my life make her passionate?" I ask, still trying to distract myself from Lucas's extremely hot body beside me.

He scratches his chin. "Do you and your mum get along?" he asks, ignoring my question.

I shift uncomfortably on the bed, no longer concerned with how close he is to me. "My mother and I have a strange relationship. I love her, but she's been hurt a lot by a bunch of different people, and she only wants what's best for me. This often means we rarely see eye-to-eye. We are close and we do get along, but I guess as the years have gone on, we don't talk as much. She expects a lot from me, and I guess I started to pull myself away the more she projected onto me. I don't know, but I do love her. I just wish she'd let me run my own life," I explain, suddenly feeling more vulnerable now than I did moments before.

Lucas reaches out, his hand finding mine on the bed. It's a simple, subtle gesture, but it carries a world of reassurance with it. His touch is warm and comforting, a silent reminder that I'm not alone in this moment of vulnerability.

"I'm sorry to hear that you've had to carry such a heavy burden for so long," he says softly, his thumb tracing soothing circles on the back of my hand. "But it's clear that you do love her, and she loves you. Hold onto that, nothing else."

His words are like a balm to my wounded heart, and I don't feel as heavy any more.

"Thank you," I whisper.

He nods. "Goodnight, Rosie,"

"Goodnight, Lucas," I whisper back, giving his hand a firm squeeze.

We lie there in silence, our fingers still interlaced.

***

Something wakes me from my deep sleep and as my eyes open, I blink a few times, trying to adjust to the darkness. Once I'm a little more awake, I realise it's Lucas's arm. Lucas must have shifted in his sleep and his arm—heavy like dead weight—is currently resting on my stomach. His arm pins me to the bed as he snuggles closer to me, his head almost resting on my shoulder.

In the darkness, Lucas shifts beside me, pulling me closer. I freeze.

If I just stay completely still, maybe he won't wake up and realise what he's doing. But, on the other hand, what if I do want him to wake up and realise what he's doing?

No, get your head out of the gutter!

Lucas grumbles something close to my ear before a deep groan leaves his mouth. I suck in a breath and close my eyes tight, wondering how I got myself in this situation.

"Rosie?" Lucas grumbles beside me, his eyes blinking in the darkness.

"Hmhm?" I reply, unable to trust my voice. When I answer, I feel Lucas's arm on my stomach stiffen and his breathing slows. "Are you okay?" I ask, feeling the sudden change. One moment he's relaxed, the next moment he's stiff.

"I thought I was dreaming," he says, confusion lacing his words.

"No, everything happened," I say, hinting at the kiss we shared. I don't want him to regret one of the best nights of my life. For the first time, I felt alive. I felt desired and I felt powerful.

We fall into a tense silence. I stare at the sliver of moonlight filtering through the window, which creates a canvas of shadows on the wall. Lucas shifts, turning his back to me as he attempts to go back to sleep.

As I lay there, I imagine how awkward this fake dating thing will become if we don't have boundaries. I can't let him distract me in front of everyone. No, I need to be at my best.

"Lucas," I whisper into the darkness. It's a little shaky, but there is a firmness underneath: determination. "We need to create a story and set some ground rules if we're going to do this fake dating thing properly."

A soft chuckle escapes Lucas' lips before he can stop it. "You sound like we're planning a heist or something."

I giggle, not expecting Lucas to say that. Usually, it wouldn't have made me laugh, but being this close with Lucas, every-thing seems so intimate. Lucas turns to face me, even though he can barely see me in the darkness. "Maybe we are," I say, in between giggles. "Stealing normality from under the noses of our nosy friends and family."

Lucas chuckles, the tension seeping from his shoulders. "Fair point, Rosie. So, what's our first rule?"

"We should establish physical boundaries." I make sure my voice sounds determined. "Holding hands, hugs, maybe the occasional peck on the cheek? Nothing too intimate, to avoid getting too entangled. It's important not to become distracted, especially in front of my family."

"Sounds reasonable," he says, trying to ignore the sudden

vision of his lips brushing against my cheek, wanting him to kiss me the way he did last night.

"And how did we meet?"

"Right," I agree, still distracted by the vision of his lips on mine. "We can keep how we met, honest: we're neighbours and only recently started talking. In terms of dating, we've been dating for four months, secretly, trying to figure out what we have."

"Secretly dating? That's a nice touch, Rosie. I like it."

"Thank you," I say, smiling into the darkness. I turn so we're face-to-face. I have no idea how close he is, but I can feel his breath on my face, and I shiver, wishing I could pull myself closer.

"What's your favourite date?" I ask, trying to find out more about Lucas. Secretly, I'm just curious about him and I'm using the fake dating scenario to find out more about him.

"I prefer the dates where we have to talk and get to know each other. I don't like going to the cinema for a first date, because all we do is watch a movie and I learn nothing," he says, not saying where he'd take me.

"I think that's perfect. Where did we go on our first date?" I ask, having the courage to ask it.

"Don't laugh, but I would have taken you to a food festival because I know you love authentic dishes and street food. Then, we would take a stroll up to the harbour which isn't too far away from the festival and then we'd have a few drinks at this amazing Irish bar to finish off," he explains it like he's put so much thought into it. *Had he?*

"Wow," I say, wishing this is real.

"What about you?" he asks before I can think too much about it.

I blush. "I haven't been on many dates, so I don't know for sure. But I've always liked the idea of a picnic in a park and stargazing. I think that's very romantic," I say, feeling vulnerable revealing my lack of dating history.

"I love that. That's our second date," he says, generally sounding like he meant it. I blush again, relieved he can't see me.

We spend the next hour discussing our fake dating history, filling it with shared memories, inside jokes, and a list of our favourite dates. I find myself engrossed in Lucas's storytelling, the husky lilt of his voice as he describes our "first date" at a food truck festival.

In the early hours of the morning, we both fall asleep. Although we are laying on separate sides of the bed, the space between us feels a lot smaller than before.

Chapter Twenty

S itting in the living room with Lucas and my mother who is completely engrossed in one of her favourite trashy TV shows, her laughter punctuating the scenes unfolding on the screen, but all I can think about is how close Lucas is to me right now.

We're sitting side by side, but we've kept a small space between us. I don't know if we've done it subconsciously, but as I spot my mother occasionally glancing at us, Lucas and I exchange a shared glance—we need to try harder. If we're going to convince my mother we're really together, sitting this far apart is not going to cut it.

Lucas extends his hand towards mine, offering it to me. I glance down at his hand before reaching mine out and our hands meet, fingers intertwining. As soon as our fingers interlace, my heart does a mini somersault as the warmth of Lucas's hand enveloping mine sends a soothing ripple through my body. His hold is firm, yet tender, and it feels right as his thumb gently strokes my thumb.

I try to turn my attention back to the TV as my mother's laughs at something on the TV. But, no matter how hard I try, I can't stop thinking about the fact I'm holding hands with Lucas, casually watching TV with my mother. At this moment, I pretend that this is real. I pretend that Lucas *wants* to hold my hand, and not because my mother is in the room. I pretend this is my life, and I like it.

Lucas squeezes my hand and I steal a quick glance at Lucas, his face illuminated by the flickering light of the television. Like me, he's watching the TV, but his face looks distracted as his jaw clenches and unclenches. Summoning all the courage I have within me—which isn't a lot—I decide to bridge the gap between us. I shift my position slightly on the sofa, allowing my body to lean gently into Lucas's side. Lucas turns his head to look at me, surprise flickering in his eyes, quickly followed by a warm smile as if welcoming me and telling me that this is alright. His arm wraps around my shoulders, pulling me closer. I lean my head against his chest, listening to the steady, rhythmic beat of his heart.

Right here, I feel content—a little nervous—but content as my body melts into his body as if it is the most normal thing. It's a perfect fit, as if we'd known each other for years, as if this is where I truly belong. We continue to watch TV, but our focus has shifted entirely. Our hands remain entwined, with our bodies nestled together in a warm embrace.

****

I'm floating, weightless in the air. My eyes flutter open, and I'm face-to-face with Lucas, my head resting on his chest as he scoops me up from the sofa.

"Lucas?" I ask, barely awake.

He looks down at me, smiling as his eyes meet mine. "You

fell asleep on the sofa. I'm just taking you to bed." His voice is a soft whisper as he carries me into the bedroom. I don't fight him as tiredness threatens to take me again.

As he lowers me onto the bed, his fingers brush a strand of hair from my face, and for a moment, his gaze lingers on me. There is a tenderness in his eyes that I haven't seen before, but I convince myself it's because I'm half asleep and I'm clearly seeing things. But then, he leans down and kisses my forehead. "Goodnight, Rosie," he whispers, his voice barely audible.

Lucas straightens, and heads to the wardrobe to grab fresh clothes. He disappears from the room, and I can feel my eyes fluttering closed again. It feels like a few seconds before I feel Lucas sliding under the covers with me, careful not to disturb me. I can hear his steady breathing, and I know he is awake. Before long, I fall back to sleep, feeling happy and content as I pretend this is real.

Chapter Twenty-One

I put on the dress a classic A-line silhouette dress for the rehearsal. It's a rich maroon colour. At the waist, there is a slim maroon satin belt that cinches the dress to my body. I have to say, I feel incredible in this dress. As I put on my gold earrings and check my lipstick in his mirror, I hear a slight knock on the door.

"Come in," I say, waiting for either Lucas or my mother to rear their heads.

It's Lucas.

"What do you think?" I ask, twirling to show him my dress. In that instance, I feel extremely vulnerable by the intimate way he's staring at me. His eyes trail my body, eating up every curve, leaving nothing untouched. His eyes follow the length of my dress, his jaw clenching and unclenching as he thinks of what he's going to say.

I blush as I watch him watching me.

"Wow," is all he says.

"Do you like it?" I ask, running my hands over the silky

material.

"I … Yes, you look breathtaking," he says, his voice coming out strained as he continues to observe me. Is he observing my body or is he observing the dress?

Either way, I feel stunning under his gaze, and I wish the moment could last a little longer.

"You look amazing," I say, moving the topic into more lighter areas.

He chuckles as he adjusts the cuffs and unbuttons his top button. "Thank you," he says.

"Are you ready?" I ask, feeling nervous all of a sudden that this is a bad idea. Once my family meet Lucas, there's absolutely no way of going back.

"More than ready," he answers.

I nod, before turning away to grab my white clutch bag from the bed and a sheer shawl which I like to use in case it's a bit chilly.

"Wait," Lucas says. From the mirror, I can see Lucas walking behind me, getting closer and closer as I stand motionless.

"What?" I breathe as he gets closer. His eyes meet mine in the mirror and he gives me a small reassuring smile before I feel one of his hands on my waist, steadying me.

"You still have the label on," he says, his voice a warm whisper against my ear. I feel a shiver run down my spine as his hands reach for the label, his touch sending a pleasant jolt through me.

Bending down slightly, his warm breath falls on the nape of my neck, causing me to shiver again. With gentle precision, Lucas places the label between his teeth, his lips grazing my skin as he tugs gently, his eyes watching me in the mirror. The label gives way, and I feel it being pulled off my dress. It flutters to the ground, forgotten, as Lucas straightens back up.

He slowly moves away, his breathing sounding harsher than before as he clears his throat. "Okay, that's sorted. Shall we go?" he asks, avoiding my gaze as he messes around with his tie again, avoiding all eye contact.

"Uh, yeah." I say, still reeling from what just happened.

****

"You look gorgeous!" my mother exclaims, shock filling her voice as her hands cover her mouth.

I look down at myself, loving the way the dress hugged my figure. "Thank you," I say, looking at myself in the mirror and smoothing the dress over. I like the dress. It's simple and elegant, and *me*.

My mother wipes a small tear from her cheeks. "I can't wait until it's your day," she says. "Let's hope your marriage is better than mine."

I want the ground to swallow me whole.

"Mother, do you have to ruin a perfectly good moment?" I ask. My mother shrugs and opens her mouth to reply. I interrupt, stopping her in her tracks. "We have"—I pause and check the time—"another hour before it starts. Maybe we should get going?" I suggest, knowing if nothing else will get her moving, the thought of being late will.

She makes a face but doesn't disagree with me.

"Are you happy with Lucas?" she asks, out of the blue. I turn to face her, the question taking me by surprise.

"Yeah, why do you ask?" I ask, answering honestly. I never thought I'd answer that question honestly, but these last few days have shown me the kind of person he is.

My mother sighs and sits on the edge of the bed. "I just want to see you happy. You know how your father treated me, and I just don't want that for you," she confesses. I haven't seen this side of my mother in years since my father cheated on her and treated her like shit, she built walls so high, not even her daughter could penetrate them.

I sit beside her, holding her hands in mine. "You don't have to worry about me, okay?" I say, finally believing this myself.

She nods, squeezing my hand tighter. "He is very handsome, isn't he?" she whispers, nudging my arm.

I laugh, not surprised by how long it took for her to go back to normal. "He's okay," I say, ignoring how attracted I'm becoming. It's not because of his looks, but he's starting to show his true colours, and they aren't what I thought.

They're better and brighter.

She wraps her arms around my shoulders and pulls me in.

My heart melts, and I soak up this moment because I don't know when it will happen again. The last time I saw my mother was at my twenty-ninth birthday party, and she was in rare form. Sitting here with her today, that woman isn't here. She's not judging or picking up on things I should be doing better. I know she does it because she cares, but *this* is the woman I've been craving.

I try to change the subject so she stops mentioning my boyfriend as the guilt starts gnawing at me.

I mean, *fake* boyfriend.

Kinda fake boyfriend.

It's complicated.

"Shall we get going?" I say.

My mother and I both walk out of the room, and the first thing I see is Lucas. He hasn't spotted me yet as my Aunt Julia, who arrived this morning, gives him a low-down on the family and what he can expect. He nods, listening intently, and my heart melts a little more.

He's standing beside the fireplace, drinking his coffee, and I can't help but notice the way his arm flexes as he picks up the mug. I watch as he takes a sip and I give particular attention to the way he licks his lips before they touch the mug and the way he briefly shuts his eyes as he takes a swig. I take another opportunity to look at him in a suit. I want to say he looks terrible in a suit and lie to myself about my attraction for him, but I can't.

"What do you think of her dress, Julia?" my mother asks, drawing Lucas's attention to me.

Julia hums as she takes me in, pulling me back to the present moment. "You look stunning! I can't wait to see you in the bridesmaid's dress," she says, giving me a proud smile..

"I think she's beautiful! What do you think, Lucas?" my mother asks, throwing him a knowing glance. Little do they know, he's already seen me, but I won't pass on another compliment from him.

He swallows hard, putting his mug down. "You look amazing," he says, his voice sounding hoarse as he scratches his chin. I blush as my mind goes back to the night he held me the way I wanted him to.

"Are we ready?" I ask, wanting to move the subject away from me.

Once everyone is ready, we head out to my mother's car. Lucas and I are in the back as Julia calls "shotgun." Honestly, I thought that was for kids, but apparently not. Lucas and I get into the back seat, and once all the doors are closed, my palms begin to sweat, and my head becomes filled with awkward scenarios which could humiliate me.

As Julia and my mother fight over which route to take. I take a deep breath, sitting back against the leather chairs. It's been about twenty minutes of driving in silence. I'm not sure if I can take it any longer.

I lean closer to Lucas. As I do, I can smell his sandalwood cologne.

"Lucas, what if people don't believe us? I mean, I'd finally be the embarrassment I've tried to avoid being," I whisper, regret and panic starting to distract me from my dangerous thoughts of Lucas. Maybe that's a good thing.

He gently takes my hand and sits back in the chair. "It'll be fine. After all, we've been practising," he says, throwing me a sexy wink. I blush, already feeling better.

He shuts his eyes, leaning his head back against the headrest. Julia and my mother continue to gossip about a few people who are going today.

Lucas opens one eye and smiles. "It'll be fine," he promises, giving my hand another squeeze.

Feeling better, I sit back again and fold my arms across my chest, staring out of the window at the beautiful scenery passing us by. I see Lucas move beside me and from the corner of my eye, I watch as he wipes his hands on his thighs and the action causes the velvety fabric of his black tux to tense, showing off his world class muscles. Muscles I've had the pleasure of getting to know. I just wish we could get to know each other more than just light fondling.

His tight muscles strain against the sleeves, and my mind brings me back to his flat. I can remember how warm his skin felt and how strong his arms were as he held onto me. As my thoughts pick up, I can remember how much I wanted his lips to crash onto mine as I sat there on his desk and how I would have done anything for him at that moment. I don't think I've ever met a man I want so much, but also want to stay away from.

As I shake my head, trying to shake off the inappropriate feelings. Feelings I shouldn't feel with my aunt and my mother in the car!

As I look at him from my peripheral, I reassure myself that it's hard to not be distracted by the giant sitting across from me. He takes up his own seat, as well as the middle seat, so we have no chance of getting a third person in this car.

He shifts in his seat, and I watch as his shoulders bulge against the shirt. He's sitting there all stoic and serious. The longer we sit beside each other in silence, I'm able to drown out my mother and Julia waffling about something. Instead, I'm allowing myself to appreciate how attractive he is. It's not like it's a new revelation and that I had overlooked how attractive he is, because I noticed.

We pull up outside the venue.

You've got this.

****

As soon as we enter the grand hall, I can feel myself start to panic. Even though it's only a rehearsal, it's the start of a lie. Lucas gently grabs my hand, as if he sensed my discomfort. Before I can say anything, Maddy comes rushing up to me wearing the most stunning white dress. It isn't the wedding dress, but it's just as beautiful.

"Rosie, you look fantastic!" Madilyn screams, rushing into my arms as she pulls me in for a suffocating hug. I laugh as I embrace her, trying not to crease her stunning dress.

I pull back, looking at Maddy with a gasp of admiration, captivated by the sheer beauty of the ensemble which wraps around Maddy. "Maddy, you look gorgeous and radiant!" I exclaim, my voice filled with awe.

Maddy squeezes my hand, her eyes sparkling with sincerity. Her eyes then flash up to Lucas who is standing beside me.

She shoots me a quick glance with a small smirk before she pulls Lucas into a hug. He stands stoic and unnatural as she squeezes him, unsure of what to do. I can't hold the laugh in as his eyes look to mine for help.

"It's lovely to have you here! I must introduce you to the family!" she insists, sweeping him away to meet our ludicrous family. He shoots me one last look, panic in his eyes as she drags him through the crowd.

As I watch Lucas being carried off by Maddy, I can't help but grin. It's a sight to behold, and I know he'll soon find himself enveloped in the warm chaos of my family's affection. With a chuckle, I decide to give him some time to navigate the crowd and head towards the bar.

I order my usual large white wine with ice. As I lean against the bar, my eyes wander around the bustling room, already losing sight of Lucas. I take in the scene of family and friends coming together to celebrate Madilyn and Sophia, and I try not to let the scene get to me. This is their rehearsal, after all.

Just as I'm about to take another sip of my drink, a familiar voice interrupts my thoughts. "Rosie, dear, there you are! I've been looking for you."

I swivel on the stool to see my great-aunt Harriet, a spirited woman in her seventies, approaching me with a beaming smile. She's dressed in an elegant, yet slightly eccentric, outfit that perfectly reflects her free-spirited personality. She's always been the aunt who dances until she's the last one on the dance floor, whilst going through bottles of wine without a care in the world.

"Aunt Harriet!" I greet her warmly, setting my drink down and embracing her. Her hugs have always been known for their warmth and comfort. She's never been the type to judge me for anything. She's always been the best for advice, and she's never been wrong.

She holds me at arm's length, her eyes twinkling with mischief. "You know, Rosie," she says in a warm tone, "I can't help but notice the chemistry between you and that handsome young man you just came in with. I just wanted to say, I'm happy for you."

I chuckle. "Thank you, but we've only just started seeing each other," I say, trying not to reveal too much.

She turns her head, and I follow her gaze. My eyes meet Lucas's who is watching me with an expression I can't quite read. "I would say he's been in love with you for a long time. He hasn't stopped looking at you," she says, giving me a knowing look. "Just do what makes you happy. Not anyone else." Before I can respond, she winks mischievously and leaves with her drink.

I look back at Lucas, his eyes fluttering from me to my family who has surrounded him. They're most definitely questioning him about us, but his attention is solely on me. As my family discusses something amongst themselves, leaving him some space to breathe, I watch as he pulls out his phone and types something.

My phone vibrates. I look at it, and see a text from Lucas.

Lucas: *How is that gigantic glass of wine treating you?*

Chapter Twenty-One

I laugh, looking up from my phone to give him the middle finger.

Me: *I need all the help I can get with this lot. Are you having fun?*
   Lucas: *I will be if you come over here.*
   Me: *I'm the one sitting by the very nice bar.*
   Lucas: *You do have a good point.*

"Rosie," my mother exclaims, walking up to me with her hands on her hips, "can you put down your phone for one minute and come help me open up the rehearsal room?"

I place my phone in my clutch bag. "Where's aunt Julia? Surely she can help seeing as she's the mother of the bride?" I ask, finishing off my glass of wine.

My mother huffs in frustration, her irritation with Aunt Julia evident. "I'd rather you help me. That woman is clueless! She put the chairs the wrong way around. I mean, who does that? Come on!"

With a chuckle, I hop off the bar stool and follow my mother towards the rehearsal room, weaving in and out of family members who keep congratulating me on my new boyfriend. I stop myself from flipping them all off.

****

Once the room is set up, ready for the rehearsal, I go out to find Lucas. Searching the crowd, I can't see him anywhere. I continue to push through the crowd, pulling out my phone to text him.

Me: *Where are you?*

I hold onto my phone in case he texts back.

I begin to wonder if he's stepped outside for some fresh air or found himself engaged in a conversation of questions.

As I near the bar, a central location I tell myself, my phone buzzes with a notification. I quickly unlock it to read Lucas's response.

Lucas: *Clue: You might find me where the whispers are the loudest.*

I furrow my brow, confused by his cryptic response.

Me: *What does that mean?*

He reads the message but doesn't reply back. I scan the room once more, seeing if I can spot him.

I don't.

Taking a moment to decipher his clue, I realise that "whispers" could be a reference to the area by the toilets, where I very often have private conversations with friends.

Without a second thought, I start making my way in that direction, weaving through the crowd, occasionally muttering a thanks as they compliment the new man on my arm.

As I approach the hallway which leads to the toilets, away from the noise of everyone's conversation and the music, I see Lucas, standing by a window just outside the toilets. It's a quiet place to get away from everyone, and I don't blame him. He's leaning against the wall, his expression a mix of amusement and slight overwhelm. I didn't expect anything else from my family. It's clear that he wasn't expecting such an intense interrogation, despite my warnings.

A grin spreads across my face as I approach him, my eyes meeting his. "I found you," I say, feeling nervous all of a sudden.

"You did," he replies, pushing off the wall. "How long do we have before the rehearsal?" he asks, his voice and his eyes softening as if I relax him.

I check the time on my phone. "We have about ten minutes before it starts. What are you doing out here?" I ask, the silence of this hallway making me realise how alone we are.

"You were right—they are very interesting people," he says, chuckling. I nod, knowing they're a lot.

"I'm sorry if they interrogated you," I say, feeling slightly embarrassed.

He moves closer. "Don't apologise. I actually think it's nice. You mean a lot to them, and they just want to know you'll be okay," he says, continuing to move closer. He scratches his chin, something he does when he's unsure or nervous, I've noticed.

"What?" I ask, appreciating how attractive he looks right now in the light which is coming through the window.

"I haven't kissed you yet. Do you think it would be a good idea to kiss once, in case we need to do it for real?" Lucas asks, clearing his voice, looking as awkward as I feel.

"Um, I suppose so," I say, not able to think of a reason why we shouldn't. It does make sense because it won't look as awkward or won't look obvious that it's our first kiss.

He slowly moves closer to me. I think it's going to be a soft kiss which lasts a few seconds, but boy am I wrong.

He gently holds the side of my face as his mouth comes down on mine. He doesn't hesitate.

It was an intimate kiss, which is tender but also desperate. My body responds to his, as I reach out, holding onto his jacket, pulling him in closer as we deepen the kiss. His teeth gently graze my bottom lip and his hand trails down my

193

dress, stopping at my waist. His hands pull me closer, gently squeezing my waist. His lips leave mine for a moment, and the disappointment is devastating. Before I realise what's happening, Lucas looks behind me, guiding me backwards until my back hits the wall. Once he's satisfied that I'm secure, his lips crush on mine again, his hands going to my hair. The world around us seems to fade into nothing as we lose ourselves in each other.

But just as quickly as it begins, it's interrupted.

"Oh, I'm so sorry!" Elijah's voice suddenly exclaims from behind Lucas, shattering the fragile bubble of our stolen moment.

Lucas jumps away from me, his hand instinctively moving to wipe his lips with his thumb. The look on his face is a mix of embarrassment and surprise.

Elijah winks at me with a playful glint in his eye, fully aware of the awkwardness he's just stumbled upon. His look also tells me that I'll be explaining myself later.

"I didn't mean to intrude on your private moment," he teases, his tone light-hearted. "But, hey, I always knew you two would make a great couple."

I can't help but roll my eyes, feeling my cheeks warm with a blush. Lucas, still recovering from the unexpected interruption, gives Elijah a sheepish smile.

"Thanks, Elijah," I reply, my voice a mixture of amusement and gratitude. "You have impeccable timing, as always."

"Always. I just need to use the loo," he says, smiling as he brushes past us. Once he's gone, I lean against the wall, releasing the breath I have been holding. Lucas and I look at each other, neither one of us saying a word.

"My face?" I ask Lucas. "Do I have make-up everywhere?"

I ask, suddenly acutely aware of my appearance. I realise I probably look a mess after his hands were in my hair and his lips have probably messed up my lipstick.

Lucas chuckles softly, his gaze tracing my face with warmth, the previous awkwardness is now gone. "You look perfect," he reassures me, his fingers lightly brushing a stray strand of hair away from my face. His touch is gentle, and I can feel my heart skip a beat at his tenderness.

Elijah comes out of the toilet, smirking as he sees Lucas fixing my hair and gently removing a smudge of lipstick from the corner of my mouth.

Lucas looks behind him, giving Elijah a polite smile before he moves away from me. "I'll give you two a minute. I'll be in the rehearsal," Lucas says. He heads out into the hall, the music and sound of conversation erupting the previously quiet space. He shoots me one last smile before he disappears.

Elijah rushes up to me and gives me a hug. I haven't seen him in a few weeks as I've been super busy with work but seeing him here now is making me so happy.

"Girl! What the hell was that kiss?" he asks, looking as happy as I am.

"I have so much to catch you up on!" I say, wanting to tell him about Lucas.

"Tell me everything," he says, pulling me towards two seats just outside of the bathrooms—so I did, leaving nothing to the imagination, and as suspected, he was shocked, but deliriously happy. I even told him about us fake dating, but that I've also started to feel something for him.

"I just don't know if he feels the same," I say, biting my nails as I unload everything onto Elijah.

"Girl, he likes you! That kiss wasn't mediocre. It was

passionate, and if I didn't just barge in on you, I think you would've done more than kiss. A guy who doesn't like a woman, doesn't kiss like that," he gushes, holding his hand over his mouth in shock. "I knew it would be Lucas!"

I shush him, looking around to make sure no one else had come in without us noticing. "I had no idea I even liked him!" I admit, feeling stupid I didn't see it sooner.

"I saw it from the day you spoke to each other in my cafe. I am not blind," he says, gently poking my arm.

"What do I do?" I ask, desperately looking for an answer to all of my problems.

Elijah leans in closer. "You tell him. He likes you, I'm telling you."

It finally sinks in as we continue back to the rehearsal.

Holy shit.

Lucas and I kissed.

I had kissed Lucas.

Lucas had kissed me.

Chapter Twenty-Two

The rehearsal had already started as Elijah and I rushed into the hall. Elijah takes his seat beside my mother and I stand beside Maddy. I watched as everyone went through the motions of the ceremony. As I stand up front with the rest of the wedding party, my attention should have been on the ceremony, but it isn't. Across the aisle, in the audience, I can feel his gaze on me like an electric current.

Lucas.

After our unexpected, stolen kiss earlier, there is a newfound awareness between us, an unspoken connection that seemed to linger. My heart races with each stolen glance I'm brave enough to take. I can't help but blush under his watchful gaze.

I fidget with the bouquet in my hands, a subtle attempt to divert my attention, but it is impossible to ignore the intensity of his eyes on me. The world around me seems to blur as I lock eyes with Lucas, the rehearsal moving forward without me.

Maddy nudges me gently, pulling me back into the present.

"Rosie, pay attention!" she whispers with a knowing smile. She, too, had caught us looking at each other.

I bite my lower lip, trying to regain my focus. "Sorry, Maddy," I reply, offering her an apologetic smile.

"The bouquet?" She asks, handing me hers. I take it before my gaze involuntarily wanders back to Lucas, who had a slight smile playing on his lips.

As the ceremony neared the end, I couldn't help but think about that kiss. Is Elijah right? Does Lucas think of me as more than just friends?

Lucas and I exchange one final, lingering look, and I feel a rush of emotions flood over me.

I like him.

I think I more than like him.

Shit, shit, shit.

****

Back at the bar, I drink more wine, thinking about how beautiful the rehearsal was. The wedding is next weekend, and then the charade between Lucas and I is up. I'll probably be back at my flat soon, and something in me hates the thought.

Lucas comes up behind me and wraps his arm around my waist.

"Ready for some rehearsal food? This is probably my favourite part," Lucas whispers in my ear. Is he doing this because he likes me or because he's my fake boyfriend for the night? Either way, I love the feel of his arms around me.

Lucas extends his arm, offering it to me. I hesitate for a moment before taking it, and together we make our way through the crowded hall. Whispers and glances follow us as we move through the room, re attracting the attention of my friends and family. We've been the topic of conversation all night. This is Maddy's wedding, and yet, everyone has their eyes on me. I feel bad for taking the limelight off my cousin, but it's not like I want it.

We find an empty table and take a seat. I steal a furtive glance at Lucas, and I catch him doing the same to me.

"Thanks for agreeing to do this, Lucas. I know it's a lot to ask," I say, nervously.

Lucas smiles warmly. "It's not a lot to ask. It gives me a chance to spend time with you," he says, gently touching my leg under the table. I blush at his words and my heart skips a beat as I'm left questioning if he's faking it or if he really feels this way.

Lucas's eyes leave mine for a second as he glances around the room. I follow his gaze and notice my family are watching us with a mixture of emotions. Some looked happy, others looked sceptical.

I lean closer towards him, trying to play up to them and give them what they want. "They're just bored with their own lives, and they feel the need to pester me about my love life. They think I'm some sort of failure because I'm still single, so me showing up with you today has blown their tiny minds," I explain, chuckling to myself.

"Well, they're witnessing the most successful fake relationship in history. We'll show them," he says, before he gently plants a kiss to my cheek.

He kissed me, but does that mean he wants me?

Before I can fall deeper into my new insecurity, my Aunty Mary approaches the table, looking rather intrigued.

She raises an eyebrow at us. "Rosie, Lucas, I must say, you

make a lovely couple. I'm sorry I haven't seen you until now. I have to ask, how long have you been together?" she asks.

I fumble for the words, distracted by the thoughts of Lucas. "About..."

Lucas cuts in. "We've known each other for years as we live next door. But we only recently started talking and love just snuck up on us. We've only recently discovered our feelings for each other. It's been quite the whirlwind romance," he explains it like he's told this story thousands of times.

He probably has throughout the night. I look at my aunty, hoping she bought it, and like everyone else, she does. She looks satisfied, and with a wink, she walks away. Once she's out of ear shot, I look at Lucas and we both burst into laughter, relieved we got away with that.

"She's so nosey!" I say in between laughs. "You're quite the actor, Lucas. I almost believed we were a real couple," I say, trying to fish for more.

"I've been asked the same question about ten times tonight. Don't worry, I got you," he says, squeezing my hand.

I open my mouth to respond, before my cousin Bella sits down beside me. It's going to be a long night.

"Tell me, how did you two meet?" she asks, rushing past the greetings and pleasantries.

I laugh at Lucas's expression before I answer. "We live next door to each other," I explain.

"Come on, there has to be more of a romantic story of how you two met! I saw the way you were looking at each other during the rehearsal," Bella says, her mouth pouting in curiosity. Bella's eyes jump from mine to my fake boyfriend who is sitting beside me, drinking his beer casually.

"Truly, we met when Lucas moved in next door. He's my

neighbour," I insist, glad that this isn't a lie. I avert my eyes from Bella's dissatisfied gaze. She turns to Lucas, giving him her undivided attention.

"Give me details then. Did you realise one day that she was the one for you? Did you knock on her door and take her in your arms, kissing her like an animal?" she asks, her eyes glazing over as she thinks about the scene in her head. I almost thought about it myself, but instead, I gently push her, stopping her from thinking of things I wouldn't want my cousin to think about.

"Get your head out of the gutter. I'm not discussing my sex life with my cousin, okay?" I insist, wanting the ground to swallow me whole.

"So, you've had sex?" she asks

"Bella, you haven't even introduced yourself to Lucas. Maybe start there?" I insist, embarrassed that Lucas is finally seeing my family for who they are. It's just rude, and I start to wonder if I've made a mistake bringing him here.

She rolls her eyes but listens to my advice. "I'm Bella, Rosie's cousin," she says, not sounding apologetic, but I accept it. It's the best we'll get from someone who hates being told off.

Lucas smiles. "Nice to meet you, Bella."

"So, now we have that out of the way, how is your sex life?" she asks again, sounding engrossed.

I groan, pinching the bridge of my nose. Before I can give her a speech on how I think she's rude and disgusting, Lucas chuckles and wraps his arms around me from behind.

"Dance?" he asks, his hot breath against the nape of my neck is enough to send shivers through my entire body.

He wants to dance? With me?

I stare at his outstretched hand, completely forgetting what

I'm supposed to do.

Lucas frowns, his hand still outstretched, waiting for my answer.

"Do you want to dance or not? This offer is about to expire," he says, waving his arm in front of my face. I chuckle and throw a not so sorry look at Bella who is staring at Lucas like he's the last man on earth. I have some satisfaction from that, so even with my heart beating out of my chest, I swirl in his arms so we're face-to-face.

"Is this part of the show?" I whisper, gently taking his hand in mine. His eyes catch mine, and he smirks.

"This isn't for show. I want to dance with you," he admits, leading me onto the dance floor. Once those words leave his lips, the butterflies in my stomach fly in a frenzy, making me feel dizzy. Ed Sheeran's *Thinking Out Loud* is playing, and at this moment, I want nothing but to feel his arms around me again.

Once we reach the centre of the dance floor, he turns to look at me. I'm not sure if it's the free champagne I've been drinking all night, but as I look into Lucas's eyes, I want to profess my feelings for him. I entertain this idea for a moment, but before I do or say something stupid, I swallow down this announcement, not wanting to ruin this moment.

Lucas smiles down at me as he puts his hands on my waist and gently pulls me closer to his firm, warm body. He takes control, and I let him. I can feel my body tingle as his other hand gently holds onto mine, leading me.

I can't believe I'm dancing with Lucas.

Lucas leans closer to me, and my heart almost stops as he pauses inches away from my lips. "I think everyone believes we're a real couple. We're doing good," he says, before planting a kiss on my cheek and pulling back.

I nod briefly, not trusting my voice. I let the music come between us, and before I know it, we're moving to the soft beat. Swallowing hard, I bring myself to step closer to Lucas, pretending like I need the extra support from the copious amount of champagne I've been sampling.

He holds my back firmer, accepting my poor attempt at being closer to him. Being brave, I place my free hand on his chest. He looks down at my hand, his eyes clouding over and his jaw clenching as we continue to move with the music. He doesn't move my hand away.

I focus on how hard and toned his muscles are under the floaty white shirt. I splay my fingers wider, gasping as he brings me closer to him, my small body encased in his bigger one. Before I know it, almost every part of our body is touching. Our whole body is involved, and I can feel his heart beating faster as I tilt my head to look up at him.

I've never been a dancer, but with Lucas's controlled movements, I'm able to follow him without thinking. It's magic, and I didn't want it to end.

Lucas pulls me away from his body, and before I can miss the warmth his body provides, he's spinning me around in a circle before he brings me back, pressing my body against his once more. This time, his hand falls lower on my back, pressing me firmly against him.

I look up at him again, and he gives me a warm smile, pressing me closer to him. I don't think this can get any more perfect, and as I let the music wash over me, I pretend it's not fake.

This.

This is what I've been looking for, and it's not even real.

I gently lay my head on Lucas's shoulder as I fully allow myself to sink into him. He doesn't stop me. He pulls me closer, humming to the music in my ear as we sway together, forgetting about everyone else in the room.

Lucas leans closer to me, his lips briefly touching the tip of my ear.

I shiver.

"I'm enjoying myself," Lucas says as he continues to sway to the music. His voice is low, causing goosebumps to form on my arms.

"I'm enjoying myself as well, even though I never dance," I admit, chuckling under my breath. He pulls back slightly, looking into my eyes with a deep curiosity.

"I thought you'd be the type of woman who would love to dance," he says, perplexed.

"Nope, I've actually never—" Before I can continue, I can see laughter forming on his face—he's being sarcastic. "Oi, what makes you think I don't dance?" I question, understanding I just admitted it, but he always knew I didn't like to dance, so I want to find out why he thinks that.

He smirks at me. "I can tell you like rules, and you rarely let your hair down, that's all. It's nice to see you enjoying yourself," he explains, his arms still encasing me.

Before I can say anything else, the music speeds up and everyone either disperses, laughing, or dances erratically to the music.

I slowly take a step away from Lucas, already missing the warmth his body gave me.

"Do you want a drink?" I ask, needing the drink after the most romantic dance of my life. Scratch that, the *only* dance of my life with a man. And that man is Lucas.

"I'll go and grab them," he offers. I give him a slight nod, not trusting my voice. Lucas heads towards the bar, and for the first time since we got here, I inhaled deeply. This peace is short as Bella makes eye contact with me and tries to weave through the crowds of tipsy dancers. I know Bella has been curious about their relationship, and the thought of having to confront that conversation makes me slightly anxious. I'm worried I'll slip up, and I don't want to risk that.

Not wanting to be questioned by her again, I rush towards the patio doors which lead towards the garden.

I step out into the cool night air, my heart still pounding from the exhilarating dance and the memories of our unexpected kiss in the hallway. The atmosphere outside is a stark contrast to the crowded and loud environment inside the bar, and I welcome it. The gentle breeze carries the scent of distant flowers and the faint sound of laughter from inside the venue, offering a welcome respite from the tension that has been building within me.

Leaning against a nearby wall, I let out a deep breath, trying to collect my thoughts. My mind is a whirlwind of emotions, a mix of excitement and uncertainty. The dance had been electrifying, the connection between Lucas and I is undeniable as I recount the way our bodies intertwined in perfect harmony.

I slowly slide down the wall and take a seat on the cold floor, unable to trust my legs to hold me up. The touch of his hand against my waist had sent shivers down my spine, and the memory of his soft lips on mine still lingers as if it just happened. I replay the moment in my mind, and I can't help but smile, feeling a newfound sense of attraction and fondness for Lucas. The way he carried me as the music sweeps around us will be forever etched in my mind.

The patio door opens, and the blaring music floods the once serene garden. I look behind me to see Lucas. As he walks towards me, drinks in hand and a warm smile on his face, I feel the instant attraction hit me dead in the chest and I know I'm in trouble.

He takes a seat beside me, our shoulders almost touching. "Hey, what are you doing out here? Need a break from the chaos inside?"

I nod, appreciating the company and the chance to talk in a more peaceful setting. "Yeah," I reply. "Sometimes, my family can be a bit overwhelming, you know? It's nice to have a moment of quiet and fresh air."

Lucas nods in understanding, taking a sip of his drink. "I get it," he says. "Families can be a lot, especially during weddings … or rehearsals like this. But I'm here, so you're not alone."

I can't help the small smile that tugs at the corners of my lips as I glance at Lucas. There's a comfort in his presence, and I feel a sense of camaraderie knowing that he, too, understands the complexities of family dynamics. "You're right," I agree, "It's nice to have someone to share this moment with."

We sit in comfortable silence for a moment, enjoying the tranquillity outside the bustling venue. I take a moment to study Lucas's features, finding his easy-going charm and the way he carries himself both intriguing and comforting.

Lucas breaks the silence, turning his gaze towards her. "You know," he says, "I haven't danced in ages. I had a great time dancing with you back there."

I blush at the compliment. "Thank you," I say. "You're not so bad yourself."

Our eyes meet, and a spark ignites between us, the same one

I felt before we kissed and when we danced. I wonder if Lucas feels the same magnetic connection, I do … Maybe he doesn't and he's just incredibly good at faking this relationship, but no one can kiss the way he did tonight and not feel something.

Seeming to sense my contemplative mood, he leans in slightly. "Rosie," he says softly, "I've really enjoyed spending this time with you," he says, his eyes flashing to my lips for a split second. It was so fast that I questioned whether it happened.

"Thank you for letting me stay with you, and thank you for helping me with this. I swear, once it's all over, we can go back to normal," I pause, realising I'm not sure I do want it to go back to normal.

Lucas pauses, his features revealing something I can't quite read. Does he want this to continue, too?

"It's okay. I'm happy to help. I'm actually really enjoying myself."

Feeling brave, I lean my head on his shoulder, relishing in his comfort. "I mean it."

He leans his head on mine. "I know. I mean it, too."

We sit there for a moment, neither one of us moving as we enjoy the quiet garden. I want to tell him that I think I'm falling for him, but I don't want to ruin what we've been building. My heart aches with the indecision as he's so close, yet so far away.

"Come on, let's go back in," he suggests. He stands up and offers me his strong hands. I take it, wishing tonight wouldn't end.

Chapter Twenty-Three

❧

The laughter, music, and clinking glasses filled the room as we toast to Maddy and her soon-to-be wife. The rehearsal has gone smoothly without a glitch and now we're celebrating with a few drinks.

But as the evening went on, the alcohol seemed to have a more potent effect than I had anticipated. I found myself getting increasingly tipsy, my laughter a little too loud, my steps a tad unsteady.

Lucas stayed close to me and I noticed, after my third glass of champagne, Lucas hasn't touched his beer. He's watching me closely, making sure no harm comes to me. He continues to discreetly check in on me throughout the night, being my anchor.

As I sway slightly while dancing with Elijah and Maddy, Lucas's hand finds its way to the small of my back, steadying me. His touch sends a jolt of awareness through me, the alcohol intensifying the emotions.

As the music shifts to a slower, more intimate melody, I find myself swaying in Lucas's direction. My steps are unsteady, but my determination is unwavering. I want to feel his lips on mine, to share a kiss as intimate as the one we shared earlier on in the evening.

With a drunken boldness, I lean in, my hand gently cupping Lucas's cheek. His eyes widen in surprise, and for a moment, I think he might pull away. But then, his gaze softens, and he brings me in close.

Our lips meet in a gentle, chaste kiss that sends a rush of warmth through me. The same warmth I experienced earlier on in the evening. The taste of beer lingers on his lips, and I can't get enough as we both sway to the music, our lips pressed together.

As I try to deepen the kiss, I become acutely aware of the stark contrast between our kisses. It quickly became clear that Lucas is holding back. His lips move with a tenderness that spoke of his care for me, but there is a line he won't cross.

Lucas gently pulls away, his thumb brushing my cheek as he meets my gaze. "Rosie," he whispers, his voice being carried away by the music surrounding us.

I blink at him, wanting to tell him how I feel. Before I can, Lucas's arms encircle me, his forehead touching mine as he holds me close. "You've had a bit too much to drink," he says softly, his breath warm against my skin. "I'll take you home, okay?"

I nod, a mix of disappointment and understanding washing over me. The haze of alcohol becomes a little too much.

As we leave the dance floor, his arm around my waist, I can't help but feel grateful to have someone by my side, watching over me.

Maddy rushes towards me, her hair sticking to her forehead

with fresh sweat from the dancing. "Are you going?" she asks. I say nothing as my head leans on Lucas's shoulder.

"Yeah, she's not feeling great so I'm going to take her home. Thank you for tonight, and I look forward to the wedding tomorrow," he says, a warm smile on his face. Maddy smiles brightly at him and quickly embraces us both.

"Thank you for looking out for her," she says. She knows we're fake dating, but I know her opinion on Lucas. She thinks he's perfect for me, and I'm starting to agree.

As we step out into the cool night air, the fresh breeze helped clear my head slightly. I lean against Lucas for support as we make our way to a nearby taxi. He hails one with ease, and we climb inside.

"Thank you," I say, pressing myself against the side of Lucas.

He chuckles. "It's okay. I'm glad you had a good time," he answers, gently stroking my hand which found itself resting on his lap.

I continue to lean on him throughout the entire car ride, trying not to throw up.

When we arrived at his flat, I felt a wave of gratitude wash over me as he helped me out of the taxi and up to his front door.

Once inside, Lucas guides me to his bedroom where he gently sits me on the bed, and feeling brave all of a sudden, I pull him down with me.

My head is still spinning, but I've sobered up enough to know what I'm doing and what I want. Everything feels strangely clear, as if the alcohol has helped me decide, and I find myself drawn to him in a way I can't, or won't, ignore.

I look up at Lucas, our faces mere inches apart. His breath is warm against my skin, and I can see the wariness in his eyes. I can tell he's still concerned about the alcohol, but there is something else there, something unspoken that lingers between us. We are both navigating uncharted territory. The chemistry that has simmered between us is now on the brink of ignition, and I can't help but wonder where it will lead.

Finally alone, and with a mixture of courage and uncertainty, I close the gap between us, my lips gently brushing against his. It's a tentative and soft kiss.

Lucas's response is tender and cautious. He doesn't reject me, but he also doesn't pull me in. He remains safe, his hands staying firmly pressed in his lap, refusing to touch me.

He allows the kiss to linger for a moment, and then, he pulls away, his eyes searching mine for understanding.

"Rosie," he whispers, his voice filling with raw emotion, "you've had too much to drink. I can't—"

I cut him off with another kiss, this one bolder, more insistent. It is a silent plea, a way of telling him that I want this, that I want him. *Hell, need him.*

For a moment, it seems like Lucas has given in. His lips meet mine with a hunger that mirrors my own. But then, he pulls away once more, his breath ragged.

"Rosie," he says, his voice a mixture of desire and restraint, "I can't do this while you're drunk. It wouldn't be right."

"I'm not drunk. Trust me, I've sobered up and I'm fine, really."

"Sober or not, you've had a few drinks and I haven't. I don't want anything happening like this," he explains.

He's right.

I nod, pulling away from him, feeling like a fool.

With a sigh, Lucas gently brushes a strand of hair away from my face, his eyes filled with a tenderness that tugs at my chest. "I'll be right back."

I nod again, and sink down with a sigh. He disappears briefly, returning with a glass of water and some pain killers.

"Thanks," I mumble, taking the glass from him and sipping the water gratefully.

Lucas sits down beside me, his gaze never leaving my face. "You're welcome," he replies softly, his voice filled with warmth and reassurance that I don't have to feel bad. "You should rest," he says softly, his hand caressing my cheek.

Lucas covers me with a blanket and turns off the lights.

"Wait, what about my mother? Isn't she coming back here tonight?" I ask, my eyes fluttering closed.

"I've given her my spare key, so she can let herself in. Your Aunt Julia is dropping her back a bit later on," he explains.

I nod, happy she's okay. "What about you?" I ask, wondering where he's going to sleep.

"I'll be fine, just go to sleep," he says, his voice warm and gentle.

I drift off to sleep, and my thoughts are a whirlwind of emotions and desires. I let them play out in my head, remembering the way Lucas cared for me tonight. I go in and out of sleep, restless as the thoughts become overwhelming and terrifying as my mind shows me what I want but cannot have. As I wake up ever so slightly, I see Lucas is asleep on the computer chair, his arms folded.

Chapter Twenty-Four

I stir in my sleep, the events of the previous night slowly returning to my mind as I think back to last night. Lucas had tucked me in, and looked after me all night. I remember he fell asleep on the computer chair, but now he's lying in bed, next to me.

Maybe the chair got too uncomfortable. Either way, I find comfort in Lucas sleeping beside me.

I slowly grab my phone from the bedside table, trying not to wake up Lucas. I squint my eyes as the brightness hurts my eyes, trying to get used to the harsh light.

But then, reality hits me like a bucket of cold water.

I promised Maddy I would help her get ready for the wedding, and I have thirty missed calls from Maddy and a lot of frantic text messages asking where I am. Panic surges through me, and I glance at the time, already knowing what I'd find.

I'm late.

"Oh shit!" I whisper, my eyes shutting as I realise I've

overslept—massively. I quietly wriggle out of Lucas's embrace, trying not to wake him. I, not so gracefully, stumble out of the bed, frantically searching for something to wear. Once I throw on a t-shirt and some jogging bottoms, I throw my hair up in a messy bun, happy that I have hair and makeup in an hour.

I make sure I grab my beautiful emerald dress and accessories, and with one last look at Lucas, who is still blissfully unaware of the chaos unfolding around him, I tiptoe to the bedside table and scribble a quick note.

Lucas, I forgot I promised Maddy I'd help her get ready for the wedding, so I'll be at the wedding venue. Hopefully I'll still be alive after she's killed me for being so late! See you soon ... If I survive!

I place the note on the pillow beside his head and tiptoe to the bedroom door, careful not to make a sound. Quietly closing the door behind me, I rush down the hallway and out of the flat.

****

I burst into the bridal suite with a mix of urgency and excitement, my heart pounding in my chest. Maddy turns toward me, her eyes wide with panic as she rushes towards me, the white silk of her wedding dress flowing behind her.

"You look gorgeous!" I say, taking in the sight of her.

Her dress is a true masterpiece of elegance and embodies Maddy perfectly. The bodice of the dress is a work of sheer perfection, embellished with delicate lace that cascades down Maddy's waist. The neckline is a classic sweetheart shape, accentuating her collarbones and adding the touch of romance I hope I have one day. The dress shows off Maddy's flattering fit-and-flare silhouette, hugging her curves gracefully before cascading into a voluminous skirt. The skirt is adorned with multiple layers of soft, ethereal tulle that creates an enchanting and dreamy effect with every step Maddy takes.

"Thank you, but where the hell have you been! You're almost two hours late!" she exclaims, her voice full of worry.

"Girl, I'm so sorry!"I exclaim, gasping for breath as I attempt to catch my breath.

I try to compose myself. "I was very hungover, and I missed my alarm," I say, hoping Maddy isn't too mad. She watches me for a moment before she decides I'm off the hook.

"It's fine, as long as you're here now. How's Lucas?" she asks, and my heart jumps into my mouth as I think back to the kiss. My eyes lock onto Maddy's with an intensity that makes her pause.

"What?" she asks, knowing I have something on my mind.

"I don't think now is the best time to get into it," I say, glancing at the hair stylist and makeup artist from the corner of my eye. I've never been the type to reveal personal details with other people around.

As if on queue, the hair stylist and makeup artist pause setting up their stations, sensing the potential remnants of drama, while Maddy motions for me to follow her to the bay window which has a bench to sit on.

"I can tell it's on your mind, so spill." Her tone is more patient now. She checks the time. "We have about five minutes, so be quick."

I take a deep breath, trying to find the right words to convey the magnitude of what had transpired between Lucas and I last night. "Maddy, last night at the wedding … something happened."

Maddy's eyes widen as she grips my hands and leans in closer. "What happened? You're starting to worry me, Rosie."

I glance at the hair stylist and makeup artist, who has discreetly resumed their work, giving us some privacy, whilst simultaneously glancing in our direction. "Well," I begin, my voice quiet, "last night, Lucas and I kissed... Twice."

Maddy's jaw drops, and her eyes grow even wider. "You mean ... you and Lucas...?"

I nod, my heart racing at the memory of his hands on me. "Yes. We kissed in the hallway, and then again on the dance floor. Maddy, it was incredible!"

Maddy let out a booming laugh, her initial shock giving way to a wide smile as she clutches my hand even tighter. "Rosie, that's amazing! I had a feeling there was something between you two. I'm so happy for you!"

Relief washes over me, and I smile back at her. "I'm happy too, Maddy. But it's just ... it's a bit complicated. We haven't actually talked about anything, and we've kissed twice."

Maddy's smile softens as she squeezes my hand. "Rosie, love is never simple. But it's beautiful and worth every twist and turn. Just give him time, and I'm sure you'll figure something out. That man definitely likes you."

Maddy checks the time again before she smirks. "We have one more minute. Give me as much detail as possible about what it was like!" she requests, leaning in, intrigued.

I laugh, but I'm excited I have a love life to gossip about. Even if it's just for today. "He took control, Maddy. I mean, he pushed me up against the wall!" I whisper, blushing from the memory.

Maddy fans herself with her hand. "I knew he'd be the type to take control. But I bet he was soft and gentle as well?" she asks, a smirk pulling at her lips.

"He was—he was both. I've never experienced anything like

it!"

"Sorry to interrupt, but we really need to get on," the hairstylist says.

As the hair stylist and makeup artist put the finishing touches on Maddy's bridal look, I can't help but feel emotional. My best friend is about to marry the love of her life, and I don't feel the usual envy I used to.

As the morning turns into early afternoon, Maddy's transformation is complete. She looks absolutely radiant in her chosen wedding dress, and tears of joy well up in my eyes as I look at her.

"You're the most beautiful bride, Maddy," I whisper.

Maddy smiles at me, her eyes shining with happiness. "Thank you, Rosie."

Now, it's my turn. The makeup artist and hair stylist asks me to sit on the chair, and they get to work. As I'm sitting there, listening to Maddy check things off her extensive to-do list, and worry about Sophia and how she is, I can't stop thinking about Lucas.

My mind is whirling with the possibility of us.

So many questions go through my mind: What if we are really good together? What if he's the man for me? What if I missed him all this time?

The final preparations are in full swing, and it's almost time to go downstairs.

Chapter Twenty-Five

W e enter the same grand hall as the rehearsal, but this time, it's decorated in sunflowers, grand chandeliers, and fairy lights. As we enter the venue, it feels as though the wedding day cranked up quicker than I expected and before long, the wedding party is lined up.

I can't help but feel a mix of emotions as I stand beside Elijah, my arm linked through his.

Maddy clutches her bouquet of gorgeous sunflowers, her hands trembling as she stands behind Elijah and I beside Sophia. I can imagine their hearts are racing with excitement, but also pounding with love.

As the violins and the soft notes of a piano begin, signalling the start of the ceremony, all eyes turn toward us. I feel a little nervous as we prepare to walk down the aisle, leading Sophia and Maddy. I can't resist stealing a glance at the guests, searching for a familiar face. My heart swells as I spot Lucas, standing in the crowd.

He's here.

As I look into Lucas's eyes from a distance, I see an intensity and determination that I can't quite fathom. His gaze bore into mine like he's trying to tell me something. His charcoal-grey suit jacket, which fits him perfectly, and the matching green tie is stirring up feelings in me. His crisp white shirt is overly tight—one of the reasons I fell in love with this outfit the other day. The first three buttons of the shirt unbuttoned and I can't stop the thoughts of me running my hands up his shirt.

Suddenly, I trip over a piece of ripped carpet that had appeared from nowhere. Elijah's strong arms wraps around my waist, preventing a disastrous fall that would have undoubtedly turned my bridesmaid entrance into a comedic disaster. In front of Lucas.

My eyes catch Lucas's again, and his once intense stare is now a small smirk as he watches me. I blush as I realise he, and everyone else in the room definitely saw that.

I let out a nervous laugh, looking away from Lucas. "Thanks, Elijah. That was close."

Elijah chuckles softly. "No problem. Just trying to keep you from being the talk of the wedding, in the wrong way."

I laugh as we continue our slow walk towards the altar. Elijah leans in closer. "Rosie, are you okay? You look distracted?" he whispers, keeping his eyes on the altar.

My cheeks turn a shade of crimson as I mumble, "I just can't stop thinking about that kiss last night," I whisper, trying to keep my lip movement to a minimum in case there are any lip readers in the room.

"It was a steamy kiss. I don't think I'd be able to forget it. We'll talk later, yeah?" He gives me a gentle nudge which wouldn't have been visible to anyone else.

I nod, and we continue our walk down the aisle, leading the way for Maddy and Sophia, who stand at the entrance with beaming smiles on their faces. Once Elijah and I are at the altar and in position, Maddy and Sophia both begin their slow and deliberate walk toward the altar, giggling with happiness as they greet friends and family.

My gaze briefly meets Maddy's, and in that moment, I see the joy and love she feels. It's contagious, and it fills my heart with warmth. Standing there, beside Elijah, I feel a different depth of emotion welling up within me. My heart swells with happiness for Maddy and Sophia, but it also aches with longing. As I feel Lucas's gaze on me, I wonder if I'll experience a love like theirs.

As the ceremony continues, I listen to Maddy and Sophia exchange their vows and rings, and I can't help but steal glances at Lucas throughout the ceremony, his gaze remaining fixed on me.

Maddy and Sophia shares their first kiss as a married couple, and the room erupts in cheers and applause.

Afterwards, I find myself at the bar, sipping on a glass of champagne, talking to Elijah. I haven't spoken to Lucas since the ceremony. We had both been swept up by multiple people wanting to talk to us.

As I talk to Elijah about Lucas and our kiss, trying to decipher what it could mean, I notice Lucas across the room, deep in conversation with my mother. They seem to be getting along, sharing smiles and laughter. It is an odd but heart warming sight.

But as I watch them, I notice something that sends a shiver down my spine. Lucas's gaze keeps drifting in my direction, our eyes meeting in fleeting, electric moments. I turn back to

Chapter Twenty-Five

Elijah, trying to give him my full attention.

My phone buzzes with a text on the bar. I pick it up and see the name "Landlord" on the screen. I open up the message, already knowing what this will be about, my heart sinking even before I read the words.

Landlord: *Hi Rosie, just wanted to let you know that the repairs to your apartment are complete. You can move back in straight away. Let me know if you need any assistance."*

Before I really got to know Lucas, this would have been good news. Excellent news, in fact. But living with Lucas has been surprisingly enjoyable. I didn't realise how much I love his companionship until I think back to our shared meals, watched movies, and take away nights.

As I stare at the message, I realise that I started to love living with Lucas and having some company. It had been a nice change from the solitude of my apartment, even though I used to love that. I feel like I've changed. Now, the prospect of going back to my repaired apartment feels bittersweet.

"You okay?" Elijah asks, placing his hand on my shoulder.

I look up, nodding and smiling so he wouldn't see how sad this news has made me. "Yeah, all good. I can move back into my apartment," I explain, trying to sound happy about the news.

"That's great news. I can help you move back in," he offers, placing a warm hand on my shoulder as if he knows how this is making me feel. "I'll leave you to it for a moment," he says before he picks up his drink from the counter and disappears into the crowd, leaving me with this message.

I sigh and type out a response to my landlord, thanking

them for the update and letting them know I would make arrangements to move back in. But even as I send the message, I can't shake the feeling of sadness.

Suddenly, Lucas appears before me, extending his hand as though he senses the unresolved tension between us. "Care for a dance?" he offers, his eyes betraying a shared sense of unease.

I accept his hand, seeking refuge in the dance as a welcome distraction from the unspoken awkwardness that still simmers between us.

The soft romantic melody fills the air as Lucas and I sway together on the dance floor. Last time we danced, it felt magical and easy. This time, it feels awkward and tense. Lucas's hand is barely touching my waist as my arms cling around his neck, weakly. My mind is preoccupied with one pressing thought.

I want to bring up the kiss—the one that had hung in the air between us for a few hours now. But, I can't find the words.

Instead, we both dance in silence.

After a few moments, Lucas finally looks at me. His once tense and awkward eyes are now warm and comforting. "Rosie, is everything okay?"

His question instantly breaks through my uncertainty as if I was waiting for him to ask the question before I reveal how I'm feeling. I take a deep breath, my heart racing. "Lucas," I begin, my voice soft and shaking, "about last night..."

He nods as if he is expecting this.

"It's just..." I struggle to find the right words, "it's been on my mind since it happened, and I can't help but feel awkward about it."

"Rosie," he says gently, "I understand. It was unexpected. I shouldn't have kissed you, I'm sorry."

I shake my head, "I'm not upset about the kiss, I'm just confused. My landlord got back to me," I continue, "my apartment is fixed, so I'll be moving back in," I say. I want him to understand that I wanted him to kiss me, and I want more. I don't want to move back if things are going to be weird between us.

However, Lucas's response surprises me. He seems relieved by the news, and my heart sinks at his reaction. I expected him to be sad, but his relief feels like a massive rejection.

I pull back. "You're . . . relieved?" I can't help but let my hurt show in my voice.

Lucas's eyes widen as he realises what he just did and he stammers, "No, Rosie, it's not like that. I'm just . . . I thought it might make things less . . . awkward for you if you have your space back, that's all."

His explanation doesn't soothe the sting of my wounded pride. I take a step back, disentangling myself from his arms. "I see," I reply curtly. "Well, if that's how you feel, then maybe I should just go."

I turn and walk away, leaving Lucas behind on the dance floor, my heart heavy with a mixture of emotions— awkwardness, hurt, and a deep sense of longing that I fear won't dissipate anytime soon.

****

I avoided Lucas like the plague for the rest of the wedding, and when the ceremony ended, I went back with Elijah. I needed space away from Lucas, because my embarrassment is at an all-time high. I assumed he was falling for me like I was falling for him, but he couldn't wait to get me out of his flat. I can't believe I ever fell for it.

I shake the thought as Elijah helps me move back into my flat. I would usually ask Maddy, but I don't want to take her away from her wife.

I called in sick to work, knowing Lucas wouldn't be at his flat today as he'll be working. As I enter his flat, I swallow down the hurt and upset as we lift boxes, carrying my possessions back into my flat. Occasionally, Elijah would flash a reassuring smile as he hands me a stack of books to place on my shelf.

"Don't worry, Rosie, this place will feel like home again in no time."

I try to return his smile, but my heart remains heavy at the thought of Lucas. I can't help but wonder if I had overreacted to Lucas's relief when I told him about me moving back into my flat. Had I misinterpreted his intentions, or not? Lately, all I've felt is confusion, and it's an emotion I realise I dislike. Usually, I'm so careful and I plan *everything* so nothing can go wrong.

"And once everything's settled, we'll have a little back-to-your-flat-warming party, okay?" he asks, trying to keep the atmosphere light.

I nod, appreciating his efforts. As we continue unpacking and arranging my belongings, moving from flat to flat, my place gradually starts to take shape again and I remember why this has always been my safe place.

As I put the last box in its designated spot, I can't shake the sadness that lingers in my heart. I've never felt this before, so I'm not sure what I'm feeling, but I feel broken.

My flat is back to normal, but my relationship with Lucas feels fractured. I can't help but wonder if we will ever find a way to mend what had been broken between us.

Chapter Twenty-Six

I still haven't spoken to Lucas since I moved back into my flat, which has been about three days. I want to clear the air between us, but we just haven't had a chance. Trying to forget about Lucas, I diligently respond to my emails before a knock echoes through my half-open door. Looking up, I see Dylan smiling from ear to ear.

"Rosie, got a minute?" he asks.

"Of course," I reply, my heart rate picking up just a bit.

Dylan enters and sits across from me, leaning forward with his hands clasped. "I'll cut straight to the chase, Rosie. Your recent campaigns with Rachel have exceeded our expectations. In fact, you've pushed our annual target out of the water! You've brought innovative ideas to the table and have shown true leadership potential," he says, his eyes gleaming with pound signs. I stop the eye roll that is threatening to make itself known.

Instead, I smile. "Thank you, Dylan. It means a lot to hear that, especially coming from you."

Dylan continues, "As you know, I've been deciding who will take the promotion of Chief Marketer, And I believe you'd be a great fit."

My heart leaps. "Are you saying . . . ?"

"Yes, Rosie. We're offering *you* the promotion."

Tears threaten to pool in my eyes, and now because of happiness. I have worked for this moment for so long. "Thank you, Dylan. This is everything I've been working towards. I can't express how grateful I am for this opportunity."

Dylan smiles. "You've earned it. And we're excited to see where you take the department next. Congratulations!"

Needing a moment to process this information, I shake Dylan's hand and share some pleasantries with Dylan until he leaves.

Once he's gone, I sit at my desk, taking a deep breath as I allow the reality to sink in.

I pull out my phone, texting Maddy and Elijah the good news. I then decide to give Rachel a call.

****

Checking the time, I decide it's about time I head off. My eyes are heavy and my wrist hurts from signing confidentiality contracts and other things to get the process going.

As I head out, the usual hum of the office is silenced as everyone has left.

"You've got to be kidding me," I mutter under my breath, as I head outside to find it's pouring down. I try to shield my already frizzy and curling hair from the unrelenting rain. I throw my middle finger up to the sky, cursing whoever finds this amusing. I swear rain was not in the forecast for tonight, so this is literally just my luck.

I pull my phone out of my blazer pocket, stepping back into

the office whilst I check the time. It was seven in the evening, and I don't want to stay in the office any longer on a Friday night.

As the rain hammers down harder, I decide I'm going to have to walk. I don't want to be waiting here all night, and I don't have cash for a taxi, so my only option is to suck it up and let the rain win. I take off my gorgeous white blazer, which I only bought the other day, and cover my head with it to keep myself as dry as possible. Taking a deep breath, already shivering from the cold air sweeping towards me, I take a step out into the rain, my blazer taking a few seconds to become utterly drenched.

I quicken my pace, eventually dropping the blazer because it wasn't a defence against this barrelling onslaught of rain. I only live ten more minutes from the flats, but I know I'm going to be soaked through. I'm *already* soaked through.

I wrap my arms around myself, trying to preserve the little warmth I have left, shivering as I jog along the road, keeping my head down to avoid getting rain in my eyes. My dripping wet hair is sticking to my face like my clothes are sticking to my skin. I forgot how uncomfortable wet clothes are against your skin. I think about Lucas's hot shower, trying *not* to think about him getting in with me.

The thought starts to warm me up as I think about the hot steam on my skin and Lucas's lips on my shoulder as he holds me against him in his strong, muscled arms. I shiver, this time, it isn't because of the rain.

A car pulls up beside me, and from the corner of my eye, I can see a window sliding down and a voice cut through the rain. I couldn't hear what was being said, and I can barely see who it was. As I squint, trying to see who it is, I realise I don't know them.

It's two men who are trying to get me in their car. My heart starts pounding in my chest as I look around to see if I can see anyone—anyone at all.

I stop walking, trying to quickly assess how long it will take me to walk home. After a second of thinking, I decide it will be safer to go back into the office and get help.

"Oh, love. Come on, we'll take you home. It's soaking out here!" They yell, their voices cutting through the rain as they follow me back to my office in their cars.

Deciding I can pretend I didn't hear him; I continue my jog down the road, trying to get to safety.

My heart races, and panic takes over as I realise the situation is getting more dangerous by the second. I reach into my bag and pull out my phone, fingers trembling as I dial Lucas's number. Even though we aren't on the best of terms, I hope he'll answer.

As I hear the phone ringing on the other end, I glance back at the persistent car. The two strangers inside are getting more insistent, their voices growing louder and more aggressive.

"Come on, sweetheart, don't be like that. We just want to help you!" one of them shouts, his words laced with an unsettling tone.

Lucas finally picks up, and I speak as fast as I can, trying to keep my voice steady despite the fear that courses through me."Lucas, I need your help. I'm near the office, and there are two men following me in their car. I don't know them, and they won't leave me alone."

There's a brief moment of silence on the other end before Lucas responds, his voice filled with concern. "Rosie, stay calm. I'm on my way. Just keep moving, and don't engage with them. Try to find a well-lit area or a store where you can wait for me. I'll be there as soon as I can. Stay on the line with me."

Relief washes over me as I know Lucas is coming to my rescue. I quicken my pace, desperately racing towards my office. "I'm heading towards my office," I say, my voice shaking. "Please hurry, Lucas."

With Lucas's voice as my lifeline, I sprint towards my office building, my footsteps echoing in the empty streets, and the rain pelting down on me like a relentless foe. The two men in the car still follow me, their sinister intentions becoming more evident with every passing moment. My heart races, and I can feel their malevolent eyes on my back.

I hear the sound of a car door opening and closing, and I run faster towards the familiar glass doors of my office building, never looking back. "Lucas, I can hear them coming!" I shout into the phone, unable to hear what he's saying back due to the unrelenting rain and wind.

Finally, I reach my office building. My trembling hand fumbles with the key card as I swipe it hastily, praying it will let me inside. The door clicks open, and I rush in, slamming it shut behind me. No one can enter without a key card, so for now, I'm safe. The fluorescent lights of the lobby flicker to life once I'm inside, casting eerie shadows.

I take shelter behind the reception desk, feeling nervous being out in the open where the can see me, my breath coming in rapid, shallow gasps. I can no longer see or hear the muffled voices of the men outside, which feels more chilling.

"Rosie, tell me what's happening!" he yells into the phone, his fear evident in his voice.

"I'm inside," I say, clutching the phone, my lifeline to Lucas, watching the minutes tick by on the digital clock above the desk.

"Rosie, I'm outside," he says, sounding out of breath as his car pulls up outside of the office building. Relief washes over me like a tidal wave, and I stumble towards the glass doors, pushing them open just in time to see Lucas spring out of his car.

He dashes towards me, rain-soaked and determined, his eyes locking onto mine with a fierce protectiveness. Once he's in, I shut the door with a slam and without a word, he wraps his arms around me, pulling me close, as if shielding me from the danger. My body trembles in his embrace, and tears mingle with the rain on my cheeks.

Lucas's voice is a soothing balm as he whispers softly, "You're safe now, Rosie. I've got you." His words and the warmth of his embrace banish the fear in me. Fear I haven't felt in a long time.

"Come on, let's get you back," he says, attempting to move me. I push back, not wanting to go outside with those men still there.

"No, what if they're there?" I ask, pure fear rushing through me like a tidal wave.

Lucas's strong hands cup my face gently, his eyes locking onto mine with unwavering determination. Raindrops glisten on his hair and brows, and the wind and rain rages on around us.

"Rosie," he says, his voice steady and calming, "I promise you, they're gone. They won't dare stick around with me here. You're safe now."

Tears mix with the rain on my cheeks as I take a shaky breath, forcing myself to believe his words. Slowly, I nod, my trust in Lucas overpowering my lingering fear. With his help, I rise to my feet, still trembling, but no longer paralysed by pure fear.

Lucas leads me towards his car, keeping a protective arm around me as we step back into the torrential rain.

He opens the car door and guides me to the passenger seat, making sure I'm comfortable before closing the door.

As he settles into the driver's seat and starts the engine. The seats are leather, so my wet clothes stick to it, but I don't care right now. Lucas is sitting beside me, just as soaking as me, and we fall into silence as we realise the weight of the situation.

I try to catch my breath as he pulls away from the office. The sound of the rain hitting the roof of the car is enough to drown out the silence, but it's not enough. I fear Lucas has seen a side of me I rarely reveal, and although it wasn't my fault, I can't help but feel embarrassed now I'm safe. Completely safe.

Shivering, I reach for the heaters. In the same second, Lucas also reaches for the dials to the heater and our hands touch for the briefest moment.

Lucas shoots me a kind smile and retracts his hand. "Sorry about that. I saw you shiver and thought you might be cold," he explains sheepishly. He rubs his bottom lip with his thumb as he gestures for me to turn on the heating.

I say nothing as I shoot him a friendly, albeit awkward smile and I turn the heating up. I sit back in the chair, trying to process the evening.

"Thank you," I say after a moment. Lucas keeps his eyes on the road, but I can see a tight smile on his lips.

Lucas's voice, firm and unwavering, resonates with a deep sense of reassurance. 'No need to thank me, Rosie. You call me anytime you're scared,' he says, his eyes still focused on the rain-slicked road ahead. There's a steely determination in his voice as he grips the steering wheel harder.

After a moment, he releases the steering wheel as his expression softens. He reaches over and gently squeezes my hand, a reassuring gesture that warms my heart. "Rosie, from now on, if you're working late or ever feel unsafe, just call me. I'll pick you up. No questions asked. Even if we're only living next door to each other."

Tears well up in my eyes, but this time they're not tears of fear or frustration. They're tears of gratitude, for having a friend like Lucas who would go to such lengths to protect me, no matter the circumstances.

The rain continues to pour as we arrive back at the building, and I keep my gaze fixed on the wet pavement, my heart heavy with a mixture of emotions. I avoid making eye contact with Lucas, not wanting him to see the lingering fear in my eyes, nor the vulnerability that still clings to me.

As we step out of the car, I'm acutely aware of the trepidation welling up inside me. The notion of leaving the safe haven of the vehicle and venturing into the darkness terrifies me. I take my first tentative steps towards the entrance of the flat building, but it's as though I've forgotten how to walk. The constant feeling of being watched has made me incredibly self-conscious, and my legs refuse to obey my commands. They tremble uncontrollably, no longer feeling like they're part of my body.

Just when it seems like I might falter, Lucas steps closer. He gently reaches out and takes hold of my arms, his touch reassuring me that I'm not on my own.

As we stand together in the dimly lit hallway of Lucas's flat, my eyes catch Lucas's, and I'm surprised by the depth of emotion I see in his expression. His normally calm and collected demeanour is shattered, replaced by a darkness that sends a shiver down my spine. His ocean-blue eyes, usually so warm and reassuring, now seem to be battling an internal storm.

We share a heavy silence, our unspoken emotions hanging in the air like an impending thunderstorm. Lucas's face is tense, more tense than I've ever seen it, his jaw clenched as if he's trying to hold back the torrent of emotions that threaten to overwhelm him. For two or three heartbeats that seem to stretch into an eternity, we stand there, our eyes locked in a silent conversation. In that moment, I sense the fear and concern he felt when he received my call, and it dawns on me just how much this situation has affected him as well.

As Lucas closes his eyes, he attempts to regain composure. It's as if he's trying to shield me from the full extent of his own fear and concern.

I break the silence, not wanting to burden him any more. "I should get back to my flat. Thank you," I say, turning to leave.

"Wait," he says. I pause, my hand barely touching the doorknob. "Stay. You're more than welcome to take a shower here," he offers, his voice showing a vulnerability I haven't seen with him yet.

I slowly turn around. "I appreciate that, but I don't want to take any more of your time," I say, the relief on his face when I told him I'm moving back in comes to mind.

Lucas sighs. "Go ahead, take a shower. I'd rather you stay here until I know they haven't…followed us or something," he says, his voice a reassuring anchor in the tumultuous sea of emotions. I nod, realising that is probably a good idea.

Without a word, I retreat to the bathroom, my mind still swirling with the night's events.

Once inside the steaming shower, the hot water cascading

over me, my thoughts become a relentless torrent. The memory of the men in the car, the fear that had gripped me, the unwavering support of Lucas—it all tumbles together in a chaotic whirlpool of emotions. I close my eyes, trying to wash away the residual fear that clings to my skin, but it lingers like a stubborn stain all women bare.

When I eventually finish and step out of the bathroom and throw on some shorts and a tank top, my heart races as I re-enter the living room. Lucas is there with fresh, dry clothes on and a tray of spaghetti in his hands. He gestures for me to sit on the sofa, and I comply, my confusion growing as to why he's gone to the trouble of cooking for me.

"I didn't want you going hungry, so I thought I'd save you some of my famous spaghetti," he explains, avoiding my gaze as he places the tray on my lap and hands me some cutlery.

The weight of his gesture bears down on me, and my heart pounds even harder. No one has ever cooked for me after a day like today … or ever. Not while I've been an adult. The realisation of his thoughtfulness threatens to bring tears to my eyes.

"Thank you," I manage to say, my voice catching in my throat. I can't bring myself to meet Lucas's eyes as I look down at the delicious food in front of me. The rich, spicy sauce teases my senses, and I take a bite, savouring the explosion of flavours that dance on my tongue. It's as if I've been transported to a world of comfort and warmth.

With each bite, my hunger becomes apparent, a gnawing emptiness I hadn't even realised was there. I close my eyes, relishing in the exquisite taste, and a small moan escapes my lips.

As I near the end of the plate, I finally lift my gaze to Lucas, who's been watching me in silence. I realise that in the midst of my hunger, I haven't spoken a word since he placed the tray in front of me. Before I can thank him again, I notice his hands are balled into fists. I place the tray on the coffee table and position myself on the sofa so I'm able to see him better.

I clear my throat. "Are you okay?" I ask.

Lucas swallows hard and relaxes his fist. "I'm fine. I ... I was just worried when you called, that's all," he admits, clearing his throat. Lucas takes a deep breath, and for a moment, he seems just as uncertain as I feel. Then, with a determined look in his eyes, he moves closer to me. "The kiss we shared the other night, Rosie"—he begins, his voice soft but strong—"I don't want you to think for a second that I regret it. I don't."

His words hang in the air, and I feel like a weight has been lifted from my chest. I was so afraid he was going to say he regrets it.

"You don't? But why were you relieved when I had to move back in?" I ask, wanting more confirmation in case I misheard. My voice is a whisper, almost afraid to believe him.

Lucas shakes his head, his eyes never leaving mine. "No, Rosie, not at all. In fact," he continues, "I can't stop thinking about it. About *you*. I thought some space would help, but it hasn't. I miss you"

My heart pounds in my chest as I take in his words. I can't help the smile that tugs at the corners of my lips.

"I can't stop thinking about it either," I admit, my mind is racing with things I want to say.

His hand reaches out to gently cup my cheek. His touch is warm, reassuring, and my eyes flutter closed at the sensation. I lean into his hand, needing to be closer.

"Rosie," he whispers, his breath warm against my skin. "I

want to see where this goes."

My heart soars as I open my eyes to meet his gaze. In that moment, all my doubts and fears melt away, leaving only the overwhelming certainty that this is where I want to be. With Lucas. I instinctively move closer to him, and I can see him swallow hard.

Please, just kiss me! I scream in my head. As if he heard my silent plea, his eyes look at my lips. In the same second, somehow, I find myself in his arms, my legs saddling his thighs and his hands on my hips, holding me harder against him. My breath is coming out hard and fast, unable to process everything happening, but I wasn't about to question it. Deep down, I've wanted this to happen. Part of me was always in denial, but right now, I'm not ashamed of taking what I want.

What I need.

My lip's part, and Lucas's hand moves to my face, running his finger along my jawline and up to my parted lips. Everything in me wanted to nibble his finger, but the one thing stopping me is the tender and protective way he's holding me. I lean against his touch, my heart squeezes in my chest as his gaze drops to my lips. He's looking at me like I'm the most gorgeous woman in the world, and I'm addicted.

I wanted him to kiss me. God, I wanted that more than anything. *Kiss me!*

"Rosie, tell me to stop because I'm out of willpower," he gasps, his other hand digging into my side as if he's stopping himself from pulling me even closer. I swallow, not wanting him to stop. Everything in this moment feels right, and whatever happens next, we can deal with it tomorrow. Right now, I need this.

I press myself closer to him, pleased when he groans. I place my lips just above his ear, surprised at how confident and certain I've become in a fraction of a second.

"Don't stop," I whisper.

That's all he needs to hear.

His hand, which was grazing my cheek, was now tangled in my hair, gently pulling it so I came face to face with him. I gasp at the sensation and the look on his face, and I need more. Our lips crashed together in a kiss which shook me to the core. Our tongues meet and we both moan. I throw my arms around his neck, and his hands hold my face, deepening the kiss. I want to burn every detail of this moment into my memory in case this never happens again.

My nails dig into his shoulder, and before I know it, Lucas adjusts us on the sofa. He lays me down on the soft cushions, and covers me with his hard, warm body. He doesn't break the kiss, and he remains in control and his hands caress me everywhere. I wrap my legs around his hips, pulling him closer to me. I grab his shirt, and tug it over his head, wanting to feel his hot skin against mine. Once his shirt is off, Lucas tugs at my shirt and pulls it over my head, his eyes hazy and his lips swollen as he looks down between us.

"God, you're beautiful," he says, his eyes eating up the sight of me. Silently, I thank myself for putting on a silky bra today.

I run my fingers along the muscles in his back, and he shivers as he kisses me harder. I moan into his mouth, needing more.

Lucas breaks the kiss, and for a second, I'm disappointed. But, as his hands gently tugs my hair, making my head fall to the side and his lips start to gently kiss my neck, that disappointment is quickly replaced with yearning. I grab his head, running my fingers through his hair as his kisses slowly move down to my chest. I shut my eyes, breathing hard as I try to process what is about to happen.

I shut my eyes, breathing hard as I allow myself to feel him—-all of him. Our body intertwined as we allowed the tension of the past few days to drive our want, our need for each other.

And I knew, when this was over, we would never be the same.

Epilogue

One Year Later

The clock on my office wall ticks away as I count down the seconds of when I get to see Lucas. It's our one year anniversary, and he's arranged something special. I don't know where or what it is, but I know I'll love it. It's my first time ever experiencing a one year anniversary, and I am so excited.

Life with Lucas has been amazing.

As the Chief Marketer of the company, I was finally in a position to make the kind of impact I had longed for in my career.

Once the clock hits "one" I shut down my computer and tidy up my desk. Being the Chief Marketer has its perks as I decide when I finish.

I grab my bag and make my way to the front desk to sign out in case anyone needs me this afternoon. I've already cancelled two meetings for this afternoon, and I've set my *"Out of Office"* message on my email. I shouldn't be disturbed, nor did I want to be disturbed.

Just as I step out of the office building and into the bustling city streets, my phone chimes with an incoming text message. My heart did its usual somersault as I see Lucas's name on the screen. It reads, "*Meet me at the park near your office in 15 minutes. Be ready for an adventure. Love you ;)*"

A rush of excitement courses through me as I read the message. With a quick response that says, "*On my way, I can't wait,*" I practically run to the park.

I enter the park and I spot Lucas waiting for me on a bench. He smiles broadly at me as he watches me approach. He looks incredibly handsome in a casual outfit, his eyes filled with warmth and love for me. My heart squeezes in my chest as the sight of him.

"Hey, you," he says, his voice sounding excited.

I practically run into his arms, unable to contain my excitement. "Lucas! What's the surprise? You've had me on edge all day!"

He chuckles, his arms wrapping around me in a tight embrace. "Patience, my love. All will be revealed soon."

Finally, we reach a clearing where a vibrant, rainbow-coloured hot air balloon stands tall, its wicker basket swaying gently in the breeze. My eyes widen with astonishment as I take in the sight.

"Lucas, is this … for us?" I ask, my voice filled with excitement.

He grins, his eyes sparkling. "Yes, Rosie. I remember you telling me that a hot air balloon ride is on your to-do list. I never forgot, I've just been waiting for the perfect moment to do this for you."

I can't believe it. I can't believe that Lucas has not only remembered that but he has gone the extra mile to make it happen. My heart swells with love for him.

Tears of happiness well up in my eyes as I throw my arms around him, embracing him tightly. "Lucas, this is the most incredible surprise. I can't believe you did this for us."

He hugs me back just as fiercely, his voice soft and filled with raw emotion. "I wanted to make our one-year anniversary unforgettable, Rosie."

We are soon joined by the friendly hot air balloon crew, who helped us into the sturdy wicker basket. As the balloon slowly ascends into the sky, my heart feels light, and the worries of the world below melts away. It's just Lucas and me.

We watch as the sun begins its descent, painting the sky with hues of orange and pink. The city stretches out beneath us. Life looks so tiny from up here.

Lucas wraps his arm around my shoulders, and I lean into his embrace, feeling the warmth of his love and the breeze on my skin. I don't think I've ever been so happy in my entire life.

"Happy anniversary, Rosie," he whispers, his lips brushing against my ear.

I turn to look at him, my heart full to the brim with love and gratitude. "Happy anniversary, Lucas. I love you."

Acknowledgments

Writing a book is hard. Very hard. But, it's also a magical and wonderful experience, especially when you have so many amazing people in your life to help you along the way.

Jamie, thank you for encouraging me and constantly listening to me stress out and panic about every little detail. You help me make my dream into a reality, and I love you!

Bryony, thank you for being an amazing friend and meeting me at Costa, helping me work out plot lines, and for helping me format this book! Your encouragement and friendship means the world.

Sam Palencia, thank you for bringing this book to life with the cover of my dreams! I am truly so lucky to work with you! Thank you for putting up with my messy deadlines and panicked emails, and I'm so excited to continue working with you.

Caitlin, thank you for editing this book. You have helped me make this book into something I am incredible proud of, and for that, I will be eternally grateful. You have—amazingly—made the editing process so much more fun with you funny in-line comments and amazing sense of humour!

To all of my friends and family, thank you for all of your encouragement, and for just being there for me. I love you all, and I'm super lucky to have you all in my life.

And, a massive thank you to the entire book community. I'm so lucky to be an author and to have incredible people like you reading my book. MY BOOK! I still can't believe I'm able to release stories which mean the world to me. I am so grateful to have you all in my life. Don't hesitate to slide into my DMs and have a chat about the books! I'd love to speak with you all!

About the Author

Stephanie Jane O'Neil is a romance author residing in the beautiful hillsides of South Wales. After falling in love with reading and writing at a young age, Stephanie always dreamed of being a published author. Stephanie was so excited to become a writer that she finished her debut novella, Picture Not So Perfect, in just 26 days, before its release later that year in 2021.

On The Market is Stephanie Jane O'Neil's second release.

You can connect with me on:

🌐 https://www.stephaniejaneoneil.com

f https://www.facebook.com/stephauthor

🔗 https://linktr.ee/StephanieJaneONeil

Subscribe to my newsletter:

✉ https://shorturl.at/kryUY

Milton Keynes UK
Ingram Content Group UK Ltd.
UKHW020650271123
433341UK00019B/1209